The Nightingale Quarter

Stories from the Derby Hospitals

Dave Eldergill

DEDICATION

This book is dedicated to all the hard working, compassionate and caring staff who constantly strive to keep our National Health Service doing what it does best, putting patients at the heart of everything it works for. Staff whose devotion and commitment to their vocation ensure that Nye Bevan's core principles remain as true today as they were 70 years ago: that The NHS meets the needs of everyone; that it is free at the point of delivery and that it is based on clinical need and not ability to pay.

CONTENTS

1   Preface   Pg 1

2   Fred's Story   Pg 5

3   William's Story   Pg 12

4   Alice's Story   Pg 20

5   Winnie's Story   Pg 27

6   Dennis's Story   Pg 35

7   Bijal's Story   Pg 42

8   Ann-Marie's Story   Pg 49

9   John's Story   Pg 58

10   Majax   Pg 66

11   Sister Winter   Pg 74

12   Gary's Story   Pg 81

13   Olive's Story   Pg 86

14   Harold & Lilian's Story   Pg 94

15   Conclusion   Pg 99

ACKNOWLEDGMENTS

Many thanks to the Derby Nurses' League and especially Joan Chester and Mary Williams for all the reminiscences. Thanks also to Revd Canon Paul Morris for opening St Peter's church to let me photograph the wonderful window from the infirmary chapel. I'm very grateful to Sharon, Mary and Steve for reading through, dotting my i's and crossing my t's. Mostly, I would like to thank all the people who shared their stories and made this book possible.

Dave Eldergill

"Stories--individual stories, family stories, national stories--
are what stitch together the disparate elements of human
existence into a coherent whole. We are story animals."
Yann Martel, Beatrice and Virgil

1

PREFACE

Dave Eldergill

Some people lead fascinating lives, having been present and involved in the great events that mark history. They are the movers and shakers, they make the big decisions and let the repercussions fall like dominoes, cause leading to effect. Others pass through and are only gently swayed by the ripples of those momentous times, still making choices, yet the consequences are more personal, more local. The fabric of our lives is woven by narrative and we all have stories. Often those tales are never reach an audience, remaining within the close confines of family and friends. Stories of love and loss, stories of brave deeds and selfless actions, happy stories, sad stories, profound stories and prosaic stories, we all have stories!

I trained as a nurse in the 1980s and was fortunate to meet and talk to so many people. People whose lives had traversed the 20th century and been impacted by the unfolding of its history. People who experienced circumstances I would not have been able to bear, and others who could recount memories which seemed to be the stuff of fiction.

In May 1987 I was part of the intake of students at the Derby School of Nursing which was situated at the Derbyshire Royal Infirmary. The hospital was opened and given the Royal seal of approval in 1891 by Queen Victoria and was located in the centre of Derby. With its Victorian statues of both the Queen and the great pioneer of nursing, Florence Nightingale, it had already been an establishment at the heart of the life of the city for a nearly a century before I became someone whose life was touched by this great architectural monument to healing.

Not many years after its centenary celebrations, the hospital's departments and wards were relocated to a new, modern hospital on the edge of the town. Now all that remains are four iconic onion-domed towers which formed the ends of what were once new and innovative Nightingale wards. They will be incorporated into a proposed development of housing, restaurants and shops, a last remnant of a century of caring consigned to being an architect's quirky addition to a contemporary space. They may even put a brass plaque on the wall and rename it as "The Nightingale Quarter". Trendy diners eating fashionable food, marveling at the juxtaposition of old red bricks and sleek modern design.

Any hospital exists as a place where the great and meaningful personal events of life's great journey are played out, a place of wondrous joy and a place of deep painful sorrow. It is an institution central to the life of the town, needed at those pivotal times. Some of us are born in hospital, we come into the world amidst its hullabaloo, secure that within its walls expert help is on hand to ease any trauma of the experience. Sometimes it is there
that we first encounter the frailties of the journey, maybe a childhood injury or the ill-health of a relative. For some of us it is the place where we first realise the inevitable destination of the journey and face our own mortality.

As a nurse I was able to be with people at some of these times, at the extremes of life's rich and varied patterns of experience. I wanted to try to recall that time and recount something of my own narrative, how I grew and changed as a person through the things I learned and the encounters I had. Nurses can tell some compelling stories and I hope some of my experiences as a student and whilst working in the profession may be interesting and perhaps even a little entertaining. But more than that, I want to be able to retell some of the many, many stories I was privileged to have had shared with me, those brief glimpses into the lives of others. This text is of course a fictionalised remembering, so I have changed names, I have combined things from different people and made new stories. There are places and events of which I have been told, that I have swapped around, that I have added to or deliberately decided to leave out. But mostly I am telling people's stories because nobody exists in a vacuum, all of our individual journeys intersect with those around us and in those meetings, history is made.

2

FRED'S STORY

I came late to nursing. Unlike some of the cohort who began their training at the same time as me, I was a few years past leaving school and stepping out into the world. I had been married for nearly seven years, I was a father of two young children, complete with a mortgage and responsibilities. I was also out of work, not knowing which direction my life should take. In the early 1980s the country was in the grip of an economic recession with record unemployment and mind-boggling inflation. I became a statistic complete with a UB40 card, few qualifications and limited prospects but no real idea of what I wanted to do other than find some form of paid employment.

At the age of eighteen, becoming a nurse was not even on my radar. Nothing I knew or understood about the profession remotely appealed, yet in less than a decade I had become quite a different person and was in the midst of a nurse education program. Everyone matures physically, intellectually and emotionally as they get older, and circumstances and choices contribute to those changes.

The quest for a career had led me to take a City and Guilds course in computer programming in the days when it was only large corporations, banks, universities and governments that had access to the huge mainframe devices that were the size of a small house. Computers, I had been reliably informed were the future but I soon realised that my mind did not work in that way. I was never going to be a Bill Gates or Steve Jobs, at the forefront of the newly emerging silicon chip revolution, but who knows where my brief encounter with COBOL programming could have led if I had been able or wanted to apply that learning to my future employment prospects.

It was however a very useful exercise for me in that I began to re-evaluate who I was and where my skills and interests actually lay. This period of unemployment, as well as being the incentive to studying computers, also enabled me to spend a considerable amount of time being involved in the upbringing of my children. I wasn't flummoxed by dirty nappies, night feeds or the "terrible twos". Cooking and hoovering were actually quite rewarding and on one occasion I even ran a Tupperware Party, (but that is another story). Difficult as it was financially, this time away from the male-dominated world of work that I had previously been in, was something that had a favourable effect of changing me to a more rounded person, someone able to appreciate different perspectives from those of many of my peers. My attitudes began to develop and the fixed notions of male and female roles became more fluid. The arrival of a new television show called "Casualty" with a male nurse as one of the main characters also undoubtedly had an impact on the way I looked at the world.

It was not only my change in circumstance that began to alter who I was. There was also a specific encounter with someone that put me in the place where I could consider such a radical career move. Near to the first flat we rented when my wife and I embarked on marital life together as newly-wed eighteen-year-olds, there lived an old man called Fred. He had retired from being a ticket collector for the local bus company and was a widower, living on his own. Old is a relative term, and to me, still a teenager, someone in their sixties was just biding their time until the inevitable and imminent shuffling off of their mortal coil. We got to know Fred, he was friendly and always liked to stop for a chat as we passed by his house. Over time, despite the huge differences in age and perspective, we became friends. He was someone whose experience of life was vastly different from mine and over the next few years, I developed a friendship with somebody who didn't share my still immature black-and-white view of the world, somebody who had lived long enough to know that there were lots of shades of grey in between. It was a friendship that helped me to grow and mature to the point where the idea of becoming a nurse wasn't as outrageous an idea as once it might have seemed. As a widower, Fred knew the tragic loss of a much-loved wife and the deep lasting effects of bereavement. At first he was reluctant to talk about "Marge" and their life together, but over time, as our relationship developed and trust grew he began to open up. This is the story he told.

"I met Marge in July 1946 and I know this is what everyone says, but it was like it was only yesterday. Me and some pals were having a holiday at the seaside and we went every night to the Empress Ballroom, I was quite light on me feet in those days, and it was the best place to meet a beautiful young lady.......

She wasn't ill for long you know, one day full of life and the next she had gone."

I found it hard to follow, Fred's story seeming to jump from telling how he and Marge had met to how he had lost her, without any history in between. These two moments of profound emotional resonance becoming blurred at their edges and bleeding into one tale.

"It was my mate Jack who asked her to dance first, he wasn't shy like me and had the gift of the gab, but she kept looking over to me as I supped my Dutch courage.......

It was hard to understand what the doctor was saying. We had gone to the hospital for Marge to get some tests done, but she didn't seem ill, just this strange lump that hadn't gone away.......

When we danced it was a perfect match, this stunning beauty, sequined and sparkling in a flowing pink ball gown and me in my best Sunday suit.......

The doctor had said there was nothing that could be done, it was too advanced, it had spread everywhere, we would have a few short months and no more.......

We went to the ballroom every night that first week and on the Friday, our last night there, I popped the question. I guess I just knew she was the one and I had no intention of a long courtship.......

She didn't come home from the hospital, they took her to a ward and I went home to get her night things, I just couldn't think straight, my mind in a whirl, and I missed my bus stop and had to walk back to the house.......

We married that autumn, after Marge's very protective father had given me the third degree on my future prospects. I obviously passed his interrogation, my intentions were honourable and we settled down to married life, living with the in laws for the first few years.......

It was so fast, Marge had settled into a more comfortable shape as time had past but now the pounds fell from her at an alarming rate. She got so very, very weak, could no longer walk and I watched her rapidly sink to a shadow of her former self.......

I do regret that we never had children but we did love to go out dancing and that became our life. We were good too, won medals and entered competitions all over the North.......

We didn't get the few months promised, only a few weeks. Even the ward staff were shocked by how fast she declined. I went to visit one evening after work and I was too late, nobody could call me, I didn't have a phone at that time but the ward sister stopped me as I went through the double doors and took me into the office and asked if I would like a cup of tea. I knew then, before anything else was said, our dancing days were over."

It was thanks to knowing Fred and his generous sharing of his painful story, that it was an older and hopefully wiser individual who decided to make this quite considerable, life-changing move and begin training as a general nurse. School had equipped me with only one GCE, which was in art. This was because, as a belligerent and rather lazy teenager, I felt I could make the effort to paint a picture but not much else. I had, therefore, to go to evening classes and take the necessary O level exams to have sufficient qualifications to be able to start. I then applied to various nursing schools, and following interviews, my wife and I made the decision that I would train in Derby. It was a choice that dramatically changed the narrative of our lives. We moved away from our home in Somerset and up to a part of the country completely unknown to us. To my Southern perspective, this East Midlands city seemed to be somewhere that was way up in the frozen wastelands of the North, as was anywhere that lay past Birmingham or the Watford Gap service area. Armed with newly-acquired textbooks, a gift of a nurse's fob watch from a dear friend and nervous trepidation mixed with enthusiasm, I started my first day in the School of Nursing at the Derbyshire Royal Infirmary.

Dave Eldergill

3

WARD 1, MALE MEDICAL, DERBYSHIRE ROYAL INFIRMARY

WILLIAM'S STORY

I'm sat in the office on Ward One, the busiest medical ward in the hospital. It's just before 7:30 in the morning and I am petrified. Andrea a fellow student, looks cool, calm and collected holding her notepad and pen and ready for handover. I think looks can be deceptive. Outside the glass window there seems to be organised chaos, the staff nurse on night duty completing one last job before coming in to give the day staff a report on the night's events. Everyone seems unfazed by the manic activity going on just a few feet away. The ward sister is adjusting her white lace cap. One of the two staff nurses has her eyes closed, psyching herself up for the coming storm, and two third-year students, whom I would soon realise are the founts of all wisdom, quietly chat in hushed tones. Is it only me who feels this rising panic? I am about to be launched from the high diving board into the deep end of the pool and I think I may have forgotten how to swim.

We are given only a few introductory weeks in nursing school where everything is alien and new. Long Latin names which seem impossible to say let alone remember and inexpert fingers which still lack the sensitivity to feel pulses in various bodily locations. Anatomy, physiology, and associated pathologies crammed from morning to night. Play acting with taking temperatures and blood pressures. Practising putting needles into oranges which in no way resemble the upper outer quadrant of a human buttock and getting to know my new colleagues. And now, in what seems to me, far too soon to be ready, I am about to begin my first ward allocation. Dressed in a uniform of a white tunic and light blue student nurse epaulets, as far as the unsuspecting patients are concerned, confused by the multitude of different stripes and colours, I am a nurse. I have also joined the student section of the Royal College of Nursing and am proudly sporting an enamel logo, the cherry on the cake. Yes, I am a nurse.

We had been warned that Ward One was the busiest ward in the hospital and it lived up to its reputation, a true baptism of fire. A nine week learning curve as steep as Everest and an opportunity to gain an, as yet, undeserved confidence. The nature of a steep learning curve is that it is easy to slip and fall back a little before carrying on ever upward and it was expected that as students we would make mistakes. Hopefully we wouldn't be in a position where one of those mistakes would end up killing a patient! In those first few weeks I did make some silly errors, luckily all very minor and long since forgotten. One incident, however remains etched into my memory.

It was emphasised again and again that a quick reaction could be the difference between life and death. We were told the telephone number we should call which would summon an emergency cardiac arrest team, and every student memorised it on day one. Peter had been a patient on the ward since long before we started and had become part of the ward furniture. A long term heart problem had left him very ill, and he was on a list to receive a heart transplant, as that was his only option other than death. His bed was the closest to the sister's office and we were all told of the very real risk of his sudden demise. On one particularly busy morning a curtain was pulled around his bed, Peter was using a commode as the toilets were too great a distance for him to walk. I looked around the curtain to check on his progress and was confronted by the undignified sight of Peter lying on the floor, pyjamas around his ankles. Adrenaline pumping, I called for help and rushed into the office and dialed the emergency number. "Cardiac arrest, Ward One" I shouted into the phone and then rushed back to Peter. Pulling back the curtain I found a very awake and alert Peter being helped to his feet by another nurse and at the same time members of the arrest team, beepers still going off, were flying through the main hospital corridor and hurrying to the ward.

I was told by a very understanding and sympathetic Ward sister, that I had done the right thing, as every lost second can be the difference between a patient who survives and a patient who leaves the ward via the mortuary, yet I felt foolish. The naive and panicky student who didn't check if his patient was still breathing before calling the big guns to the rescue. But what a way to learn responsibility, to have to be responsible from the first day, when the consequences of making a wrong decision are so profound.

The shift pattern allowed for an overlap of early and late staff during the afternoons and even in the hectic maelstrom of male medical, we had time to get to know our patients. We could sometimes in that less busy time chat a little and hear some of the fascinating life stories that helped to remind us that the third bed down on the left was not just "the myocardial infarction on bed rest and regular observations" but William aged eighty four with a wife, children and a story which had led him here, to be cared for, on Ward One.

William had lived in Derby his whole life and was born in a small terraced house not far from where he now lay in the Royal Infirmary. He could remember the First World War but was too young to be called up. He recalls an older brother, Frank, who was lost at the battle of Passchendaele and as I talked with him, more than seventy years later, his voice strains against the emotion as he recounts his mother's anguish and tears. William had a way with words, a phenomenal memory and a lifetime of tales to tell. He told me a story that had begun 46 years previously, in 1941, and it has remained with me ever since.

"I was working as a fitter at Rolls-Royce, we used to make the Merlin engine and that was the engine that won us the war. I worked for Royce's man and boy and I was there all throughout the duration. We were very lucky at the works, the Luftwaffe only ever managed to drop one bomb and everyone reckoned it was the fantastic camouflage that completely fooled Jerry. The rest of Derby wasn't so fortunate and there was a terrible raid in the January of 1941. I had been on nights, the factory worked round the clock making those Spitfire engines, and I only saw the effects of the raid as I rode my bike home the next morning. We lived in a small terraced house in Canal Street just across the way from here and it only took me about ten minutes to cycle home from the works on Nightingale Road. I saw a few gaps in rows of terraces, piles of rubble and splintered wood that used to be somebody's home but back then during the war we just got on with things. I felt differently when I saw my house, at least what was left of it, and I hoped and prayed that my wife Maud had been in the shelter. My home was nothing more than brick dust and broken crockery, all that was left of my comfy armchair was a torn and charred cushion, horse hair spilling out onto the road. There was Maud, walking towards me and as I breathed a sigh of relief all I could say to her was "Ey up me duck, look what they did to our house". I was so relieved that Maud was uninjured that the trauma of our home being blown to smithereens was something that we both seemed able to take in our stride. In fact the thing that bothered me most was there was no sign of the photo we had of my late brother Frank. He was dressed in his best uniform and had stared back at us from his prominent position on our sideboard for over 20 years. A poignant reminder of the wasted potential of a whole generation, forever young as I gradually succumbed to the ravages of time. There was nothing we could salvage from the smouldering debris that was once home so we left, stayed with Maud's sister and got on with our lives".

I noticed that William was becoming very tired and at that moment Andrea arrived at the side of the bed pushing the tea trolley. Those were the days when part of a nurse's job was to make a huge pot of the healing liquid every afternoon and give all the patients a real china cup of the cure-all beverage. We helped William to sit up in his bed and passed him his tea and carried on down the ward. I was very soon called away from tea duty as a new patient needed help with changing a pyjama top over a saline drip. Afternoon passed into evening and another tiring yet rewarding shift drew to a close. I didn't get the chance to chat any further with William before the shift ended and I hoped I would be able to hear the end of his tale when I was next at work in a couple of days time.

On a medical ward, a patient's condition can improve and they go home or it deteriorates and they are either moved to an intensive care ward, or they die. There were 34 beds on Ward One at the Derbyshire Royal Infirmary and after having two days away from the ward, quite a few of those 34 beds would have different occupants on your return. I started back a couple days later on a late shift and glanced up the length of the Ward before sitting down in the office ready for the report from the staff nurse in charge of the morning shift. William's bed contained another patient, a much younger man, sitting up and talking to Karen, one of the hard working auxiliaries who was kneeling down and emptying a very full catheter bag. During the handover I discovered that William had died the previous night at around 4am. This information was relayed in a matter-of-fact tone, not that the staff nurse telling us didn't care but rather that everything was kept on a professional footing. Caring is a prerequisite of the job but getting too emotionally involved hinders the nurse from being able to deliver that care to everyone on the ward who needs it. It is a fine line to walk, too dispassionate and you are ineffective and not motivated to do the job but if you become too attached the emotional strain would render one just as useless to your patients. It is a balance that is almost impossible to teach but is gradually learned on the ward and whilst doing the job.

The next morning, I saw the staff nurse from night duty and she handed me a sheet of paper. "William asked me to give this to you the evening before he died" she said and there was the end of William's story scrawled in spidery handwriting on the back of a fluid balance chart.

"Years later, long after I had retired from work, I was at a church fete. It was a glorious summers day and in between the cake stall and tombola, I was browsing through a huge collection of donated bric-a-brac. I remember I was particularly looking for toy cars to give to my grandson. Then I saw it, under a pile of used railway magazines, Frank's ever-youthful face looking up at me. I couldn't believe it. How did he end up here? Where had he been? "How much for the framed photo?" I asked the church warden who was manning the stall. I would have paid all my pension to bring Frank back, but all that was needed was a sixpence. "Who gave this to the sale?" I asked, but the warden had no idea. Where he had been since that morning in 1941 would forever be a mystery. It didn't matter. He was home."

As students, we had spent over two months on this our first ward allocation. We were not supernumerary but an essential part of the team and we were needed to ensure that patients were well looked after whilst on the ward. We very quickly developed proficiency in some of the essential practical tasks, perfect hospital corners on a newly-made bed, how to avoid spilling the contents of a bed pan on the way to the sluice and how to tell the difference between an oral and rectal thermometer. Listening through a stethoscope to the sound of the blood pumping as the cuff of a sphygmomanometer was released became, with constant practice, so much easier to hear than it ever was during our first few weeks in nursing school. Whilst making notes during report, the shorthand quickly became second nature. CVA for cerebrovascula accident or stroke, MI for myocardial infarction or heart attack, UTI for urinary tract infection and many, many more. The tutors in school had begun to teach us the anatomy, physiology and pathology of various body systems but as we nursed patients suffering from the diseases of the heart or lungs or digestion we were able to understand how the everyday activities of life could be impacted by illnesses. Somebody struggling for breath because the short journey to the day room was too much, demonstrated the lack of oxygen caused by cardiac failure in a way that theoretical learning never could. The experience of Ward One felt like starting the journey into nursing by hitting the ground and running at full pelt. We all learned so much so quickly and when in my last few days on the ward, a patient called out "Nurse" I was able to turn around and respond, knowing they were talking to me.

4

WARD 15, MIXED SURGICAL, DERBYSHIRE ROYAL INFIRMARY

ALICE'S STORY

It is difficult to imagine now, in an era of keyhole surgery and day case procedures, the length of time that a patient used to spend recovering in hospital following an operation. A surgical procedure could require a hospital stay of anything from a few days to sometimes weeks. That length of time on the ward gave nurses the opportunity to get to know their patients in a way that admitting a patient in the morning and discharging them the same evening, couldn't possibly do. There was time to listen to worries and concerns, provide reassurance because we were aware that healing involved more than just the physical wound knitting together enough to remove stitches but entailed a more complete and holistic process of recovery.

Ward fifteen was a general surgical ward but with an emphasis on looking after patients under the care of the hospital's two consultant urologists. Although it was a mixed ward the design of separate six-bedded bays meant that male and female patients were not recovering next to each other. Brimming with confidence from our first allocation, the change to a surgical ward couldn't be too difficult. After all we were now nurses!

The ward staff were used to the constant flow of new students through what was, to them, a familiar working environment. Mostly the staff were helpful and supportive to the new recruits but that did not prevent the students often being the butt of numerous practical jokes. These were jokes as old as the profession of nursing itself, and if any of the students had read one of the many accounts of life as a nurse that have been published, then they would have been forewarned of what was to come. One of my unfortunate colleagues (and I would say it was a colleague and not me because I'm writing this and I get to choose), was asked by the ward sister to go down to the operating

21

theatres and ask one of the theatre staff if she could collect two fallopian tubes for Ward 15. In defence of the student, this was early in our training and reproductive anatomy was not a subject that had yet been covered in school, something well known to the Ward Sister. So the lift was taken down to the operating theatres and the bell was rung. The operating rooms were a mystical place only entered by the favoured few and the doors were always locked. The request for the tubes was made to the nurse who opened the door. Straight faced she went back into the hallowed sanctum to fetch the items asked for. Proudly carrying back to the ward a couple of suction tubes of which there were already many in the ward's clinical room, it took a little while before the unlucky stooge realised why everybody was laughing!

There was a whole new set of procedures to learn, and not just new skills but also the rationale behind the tasks we performed. We took patients down to theatre and were allowed into that sacred space with its mystique and unique disinfectant smell, but only as far as the anaesthetic room. We placed our patients into the care of the theatre team, checking the wristband to make sure that Mrs Jones due for a thyroidectomy didn't end up having her appendix removed. Everything on the list was checked:
- Did the patient have dentures?
- Were there loose teeth or crowns?
- Any allergies?
- Had the consent form been signed?
- Was there any jewellery that needed to be removed?
- Had the patient been "nil by mouth"?

A strict protocol was followed and if nothing was forgotten then hopefully no mistakes were made.

Alice had been suffering the acute pain caused by gallstones, and ticked all the boxes for cholecystitis. She was "fat, fair and in her forties" and was in hospital to have her gallbladder removed. Her operation was quite routine, and she was brought back to the ward from the theatre complete with a small drainage t-tube protruding from the wound. Another interesting aspect of patients' post-operative care for us student nurses to learn about.

Alice was making a good recovery from her cholecystectomy, the wound was healing well, there was no infection and she was gently mobilising around the ward, to and from the toilets and down to the day room to watch a little television. It was a quiet afternoon as our ward was not on surgical take. Any acute abdomens admitted from casualty on that day were being taken to another surgical ward and I was again on tea duty, pushing the trolley into the day room to see if any of our walking wounded would like a beverage. The television, mounted up on the wall was showing a programme bemoaning the state of English football in the 21 years since the famous World Cup win of 1966, but nobody was watching it as only Alice was in the day room and she had her head in her hands and seemed to be upset. It's not uncommon after surgery to sometimes feel a little down and kneeling down next to her I asked her if she was ok. Turning her face towards me, with tears streaming from her eyes, she managed to say between the sobs, "That damn World Cup!" The ward wasn't busy, there was time to sit with Alice and let her tell her story and it seems not everyone in England was happy on that afternoon in July 1966 when Bobby Moore held the Jules Rimet trophy aloft.

"I met Bob in 1964, I was only 18 and he was a little older than me. It wasn't love at first sight, I made him have to

23

woo me and he did, quite a charmer was Bob. On our first date he took me to see the Beatles, you know the film A Hard Day's Night. There used to be an Odeon Cinema on St Peters Street back then and it was absolutely packed with hundreds of screaming Beatles fans. We held hands sitting at the back and I don't think I saw much of the film but I've always like the Beatles since then. I really fell for Bob over the next couple of weeks, head over heels in fact, and in a few months Bob had got down on one knee and proposed and we began planning our wedding. I worked in Woolworths and Bob had a good job at the British Rail engineering works so we started to save for our big day in two years' time.

  Bob was passionate about his football, he would go to every home game at the Baseball Ground even though his team, Derby County were only a second division side. And as I was always working on a Saturday, we did our courting on Sunday afternoons; trips up to the Peak District on the back of his Triumph. By the spring of 1966 our plans for the wedding were beginning to take shape. The date was set, the church was booked, Saturday the 30th of July at 3pm in the afternoon, and I started to get very excited although also very nervous. Unfortunately those nerves got worse and worse, the weeks passed by, the days got longer and I began to wonder if we were doing the right thing. I loved Bob, but was I ready to spend the rest of my life with him? That nagging little doubt started to eat away at me. I confided in Sheila, my best friend since we were at school, but she said "Everyone has doubts, it's just your nerves". The day grew closer and closer and poor old Bob didn't have a clue about my increasing reluctance to go through with it, he was oblivious, his mind completely occupied with not our wedding, but the forthcoming World Cup Tournament.

The preparations carried on, dresses for me and my bridesmaids bought and paid for, invites written, whilst all the while my internal panic was growing and growing. I went out with a few of my girlfriends about a week before the day, just for a few drinks and a chat, but I had one too many babychams and it all came out. I think I cried like a baby. Afterwards, I felt so much better; . What had I been worrying about? Of course I wanted to marry Bob! It was as though a weight was lifted from me. The morning came, overcast at first but as time wore on the sun broke through, it was going to be a lovely afternoon to get wed. Everyone was surprised at how calm I was, mum flapping around in a panic, dad practising his speech but I took my time, this was my day, I was sure about what I was doing, it would be a wonderful day.

My first clue that all was not well was as we pulled up at the church. Jack, the best man, was at the gate, "Go round the block again he's not here yet" he was saying as his arms were wildly waving the car on. Again five minutes later, the car slows down by the church and Jack is still there, anxiously looking into the distance for any sign of the missing groom. Bob it seems, decided at the last minute that he couldn't miss the World Cup Final even though his only option was to watch it in black and white on a mate's television. No soul-searching, no agonising about the rest of his life like me. No, for him it was just a quick choice on what was actually important and it turns out it was football and not me."

Poor Alice. Seeing that programme had triggered a very unhappy memory. But later, she had met someone else, someone who had absolutely no interest in sport at all, she got married and now had two teenage children who were coming in to visit that evening. Patients like Alice made surgical nursing a very satisfying experience. The rewards gained after finishing a busy shift were in some ways very similar yet also very different from those in medical nursing. The norm on ward 15 was to admit an anxious patient for what, to us, seemed like a routine procedure. For most patients however, unfamiliar with the hospital environment, it could be a major and nerve racking undertaking . We would comfort, calm down and hold someone's nervous, moist hand whilst walking next to them as they were transported on the theatre trolley. We would constantly provide the reassurance that they were in safe hands whilst making sure that their modesty and dignity were protected . We were there when they came back to the ward after the operation. We administered pain relief, made them comfortable and ensured that the recovery was progressing without complications. We saw most of our patients gradually get better and return to health, able to do for themselves the tasks with which they had needed our help during the post-operative period.

Surgical patients usually got better once an offending appendix or gall bladder was removed. We watched them walk from the ward, cured and in good health, ready to resume their lives and happy to leave us behind. Surgical nursing often allowed for a different perspective from what we had learned on the medical ward.

5

WARD 14, HEALTH CARE OF THE ELDERLY, DERBY CITY HOSPITAL

WINNIE'S STORY

Our first ward placements were over, and we returned to the school of nursing. This was quite a contrast to the experience of working on wards. No need for a 7:30am start on an early shift but a much more reasonable 9 o'clock in the classroom. We had a leisurely hour for dinner and then were back home, head full of new knowledge, by 5pm. It was a chance to see the rest of the group of students again and compare notes. We would hear horror stories of some people's experiences but would also be envious of what others had already seen and done.

We continued the theoretical aspects of training, particularly those which would be relevant to the next ward allocation: health care of the elderly. On one day in school the tutor gave us a task to try to help us to experience something of what the ageing process can do. I had to wear glasses smeared with Vaseline to mimic the effects of cataracts, and put cotton wool in my ears to make me almost deaf. Small stones were placed in my shoes and walking became slow and painful, and movement further limited by restricting my legs with loosely tied clothing. I then had to place my trust in one of the other students to guide me across the room. A crude but quite effective exercise.

The late 1980s was a time when changes to nurse education were being seriously considered. Pilot studies of a new idea called Project 2000 were being rolled out, although not at this stage in our school in Derby. Nursing was to become more academic, to be university based and given what was considered by some to be a higher, more professional status. I wonder if this emphasis on classroom-based education has been at the expense of the practical and compassionate nature of nursing. In the attempt to raise standards, has nursing become a sort of medicine-lite, with the discipline of nursing, supporting the patients' activities of daily living, relegated behind a medical model? It is a concern if very basic but essential aspects of patient care such as eating, drinking, toilet needs and hygiene are not sufficiently considered because nurses are too busy applying their equally but not more important medical skills.

This was going to be my first Christmas as a nurse. Being at home with all the family over the festive period was no longer a given, as hospitals don't close down just because it's Christmas. I had moved away from the Derbyshire Royal Infirmary and was now based at the Derby City Hospital for the next student allocation. I was to be on Ward 14, health care of the elderly or as I had always thought of it, Geriatrics. What's in a name? The latter does seem to be more pejorative, but the medical consultant under whose care all the patients were admitted, had the title of Geriatrician.

Christmas morning and I'm allocated to do an early shift. The Charge Nurse on the ward has decided that the late shift can start work slightly later than normal and the early shift can finish a little sooner than usual. There will be no afternoon staff overlap so I will be home for a late Christmas dinner. The ward is quieter than usual, as anybody able to be discharged, has been discharged. Outside, the Salvation Army Band are playing carols and a solo trumpet sings out the melody of Once in Royal David's City. I may not be at home with the family until later, but it feels like Christmas all the same.

Today I am working with Carl, an Enrolled Nurse who had come to England from Jamaica more than twenty years previously. At six foot three and heavily built, he was a gentle giant and the embodiment of care and compassion.

Dave Eldergill

The ward doors swing open to the sound of his booming voice. "Ho ho ho". There he is dressed as Father Christmas, complete with white beard, vivid in contrast against his ebony skin. The patients who have remained on the ward as they are unable to go home or have no home to go to, are each given a small gift of talc or soap from this jovial, unexpected Santa. It is a privilege to be here at Christmas.

Ward 14 seemed in many ways to be similar to our first medical ward except that all our patients were over seventy years of age as opposed to only ninety percent of them being in that age group. As well as necessary medical care for acute conditions, there was also a great emphasis on enabling the patients to be able to cope back at home. This entailed very close cooperation with other members of the hospital health care team - physiotherapists, occupational therapists, speech therapists - and also liaison with outside agencies such as social services.

On the other side of the road, opposite the City Hospital, was the Manor Hospital. This hospital was in the process of closing down, and the last few remaining patients were being transferred to the more modern wards at the City. The group of nursing students who began their training just before us, completed their health care of the elderly allocation at the Manor, as it had for many years, been Derby's geriatric hospital. It was a building that was constructed in the 1870s and before its incarnation as a hospital, was originally the Derby Workhouse. This fact was not lost on many of patients who were cared for there, some of whom had lived long enough to remember it when it was that much dreaded institution.

Winifred was one such patient, and she still had vivid

memories of the workhouse. Winnie, as she liked to be
known, (it was always a good idea to find out how the
patient liked to be addressed and not just rely on the name
written in the notes) had been admitted to the ward via her
GP, his letter stating that she had "gone off her legs." This
non-specific diagnosis covered a multitude of conditions
but basically, Winnie had fallen at home and was not coping
looking after herself. Winnie was very relieved that she had
been admitted to our ward and not over the road at the
Manor and whilst she was with us I learned something of
her story and the reasons behind her fear of "going to the
workhouse."

Winnie was a Victorian baby, born in the last year of the
nineteenth century, in a society that had very different
attitudes from those of today. Despite being very poor,
Winnie recollected a happy and carefree childhood in
Derby's West End, but that ended when at the age of
thirteen she entered domestic service with a local, newly-
rich middle class family. Hers was not the life downstairs as
one of a large group of staff in a grand stately home but
rather she was the sole servant to a corpulent factory
owner, his humourless wife and two obnoxious teenage
boys. The boys fortunately, were usually away at school.

She had been with the family for over two years when,
(Winnie was very reluctant to go into any details at this
point) she found that she was pregnant. Winnie was of
course to blame, she was the fallen women, the girl with the
loose morals and was immediately let go from her
employment. She went home to her parents, but was
another mouth to feed and not able to contribute anything
to the household so was forced to leave. Destitute, her
condition becoming more obvious, her only option was to
go to the Derby Workhouse with all the shame and

hardship that that entailed.

Events from more than seventy years previous were etched like deep scars on Winnie and she struggled with the next part of her story. She wasn't allowed to see her baby and wasn't even told if it was a boy or girl. As soon as the umbilical cord was cut, mother and child were wrenched apart. The imaginings of who the child was, who it would become were Winnie's first considerations on waking and last thoughts before sleep for the rest of her long life.

Winnie didn't want to remain forever at the workhouse but how could she find another position? Who would employ someone unable to provide a reference from her previous employer? Her salvation came with the outbreak of war. The slaughter and carnage of World War One were for Winnie the opportunity to find work in a munitions factory and a chance for her to begin again. The sons of her first employer, William and George, (and she told me their names through gritted teeth,) did not survive the conflict. Both brothers, she told me, were killed on the first day of the Battle of the Somme. A day etched in the nation's collective consciousness where so many lost their lives. For Winnie's former employers it was a particularly cruel and bitter blow: their only children and all their potential, wiped out in one awful day.

Many years later, Winnie did marry although she never had any more children, another consequence of that miserable sojourn in that hated place. She stayed in Derby for all her life, living eventually in one of the newly-built houses that replaced the slums where she had spent those early, happy years. She lived through the inception of the welfare state, the beginnings of the NHS and even had a minor operation at the Royal Infirmary in 1957. The Victorian world she was born into had disappeared, its values and norms changing in so many ways. Unlike many of her generation, she did not believe that life was so much better when she was young. Hers was not a nostalgic view through rose-coloured glasses, but a tragic and deep wound that time could never completely heal.

Memories of the workhouse haunted Winnie and when frailty increasingly began to affect her, she felt it casting its grim shadow over her again. She knew of course it was no longer a workhouse, it was a hospital, a place of care and compassion, but deep within her was a very real sense of what it had been. What had happened to her there all those years before, coloured the way she looked at the place and she dreaded the prospect of ever going there again. She had managed to stay within her own four walls, through her ever-worsening health by a process of sheer determination and only succumbed after her doctor had assured her that she would not have to go to the Manor Hospital when she was no longer able to cope at home.

Gradually as our time working on the wards accumulates, our understanding of what it means to be a nurse increases. Wearing the uniform is becoming less strange and more normal. Experience as well as text books is a great teacher. This is still only the first year of training and whilst being acutely aware of how much there is to learn, I am feeling more at ease in a ward environment. My confidence is growing and when I finish a shift I know that I have in some way been a small cog in the great NHS wheel, part of what keeps the organisation going. More importantly, I am beginning to realise that what I am doing is having a positive effect on the individual people I meet. A smile goes a long way to putting someone at their ease. Knowing to change the position of someone who is bed-bound so that they don't get sore; fetching a bedpan when asked and before it is too late are all as important as knowing the correct dose of a drug to give or how to put up an intravenous infusion. It is very satisfying and rewarding to believe that what we do, makes a difference.

6

NIGHT DUTY, DERBYSHIRE ROYAL INFIRMARY

DENNIS'S STORY

I am walking down the main hospital corridor. This is usually a hive of activity, awash with doctors, nurses, admin staff, physiotherapists and radiologists. Patients and visitors, lost and bewildered, may be scanning the signs to find an obscure location. Others may be following the red line or the white line, asking a porter and then deftly dodging an oncoming wheelchair. Normally this would be a pedestrian thoroughfare as busy as a bank holiday motorway.

But not now. All is quiet, eerily quiet, not another soul around. It is 3 am and anyone with any sense is tucked up, safe and sound in bed as I go to get myself a sandwich and cup of tea. It is my first allocation of night duty, and this is the fourth night of an eight night stretch. As students we will work a fixed pattern of nights, eight shifts on and then six off. The body clock completely resets, day is night and night is day. When I get home in the morning I have a lovely curry to look forward to for breakfast.

I am back on a medical ward and the staff nurse I am with tonight, works occasional shifts to fit in with the needs of her children. If the ward is quiet, she will take her two allocated breaks together, go to the ward's day room and sleep. She effortlessly wakes as her break ends with no need of a wake up call, refreshed and ready to continue. On my first night, I tried to catch a power nap during my break, but on awaking was fit for nothing and desperate to shut my eyes again. I can only cope with these eight nights by getting a good eight hours of restful sleep during the day and then getting up at six in the evening ready for toast and cereal whilst the rest of the family eat their tea.

The ward is a different place at night. There are no patients being wheeled away by a friendly chatty porter off the ward for some form of investigation, no ever-vigilant pharmacist checking if the doctor's handwriting is legible on the drugs chart, no self-important consultant leading his trailing minions from bed to bed on his round. The lights are dimmed and we talk in hushed tones. Mr Jones has a blood transfusion running and needs regular checks. These we do as quietly as we can but it is difficult not to disturb him when he has to be monitored so frequently. Mr Smith is at risk of pressure sores and our regular turning him from side to side unfortunately keeps waking him. We have a patient admitted from casualty and it is almost impossible not to wake other patients on the ward as he is brought in on a trolley with very squeaky wheels.

Not every patient wants to sleep. Dennis has a lot on his mind and wants to talk. He is only fifty-three and has terminal lung cancer. He is in hospital for a regime of chemotherapy, no chance of a cure but hoping to extend the time he has left. He has smoked since the age of fourteen, his doctor has told him he must stop but in the middle of each night that I am on duty, he asks me to take him in a wheelchair to the day room, shut the door and let him enjoy a furtive cigarette. Maybe, in my nurses role as a health educator, I should refuse, and tell him that smoking will kill him. This he already knows, because it already is! I decide that I'm not going to deny him this pleasure with the limited time that he has left. And during those times we share together he tells me something of his story.

Dennis believes the world has undergone a huge change since he was young. Every generation is different from the one that went before. We are not our parents but we inherit a way of looking at the world from them, tempered and formed by our own experiences of life, school, work, and friends but also greatly influenced by our upbringing. Dennis tells me he is more like his father was than he cares to admit, he shares a respect for tradition, and a deeply held belief in the given hierarchy of the world he grew up in. But with his children there has been a massive shift, their view of the world is so unlike his that he thinks it is more than just the natural progression of one generation to another. A fracture in the continuity of society. He is well read, and uses the term "paradigm shift". " I can tell you exactly when it happened " he said " because I was there."

"I come from a long line of military men, Dad was a Major in the guards regiment and he was lucky, he survived the war. His father before him was a career soldier so I guess it was in my blood. I did however have my little bit of teenage rebellion and rather than go to Sandhurst as my father and grandfather had before me, I enlisted in my father's Guards regiment, the Grenadiers in November 1954 as an ordinary private and went to the Guards Depot at Caterham Barracks. Joining the army was my chance to go anywhere in the world and after basic training I was posted to the 2nd Battalion in Germany.

In the army they say never volunteer for anything, but I did. I requested and was accepted to join the elite airborne forces. After completing my parachute training I found myself in Cyprus, slap bang in the middle of a terrorist campaign. It always depends on which side you are on but as far as we were concerned, EOKA were a guerrilla organisation and our job was to contain them and maintain the peace. The insurgents fighting against us, thought of themselves as freedom fighters, and when they killed a British soldier they believed it was a justified act in the struggle against their colonial oppressors. Nothing it seems is simply black and white. At the time though, it did seem simple, they were the bad guys and I was on the right side. Of course, I had grown up in a military family so it is not surprising that I looked at things in a very particular way. I was proud of what we were doing, we were the British Army. Only ten years previously, we had defeated the Nazis and here we were again, defending what we believed in, standing up for what made Britain great.

It was therefore not surprising then that it was through that lens that I looked at what happened next. From Cyprus I was sent to Egypt as part of Operation Musketeer, Britain's response when Nasser decided to rebel against his previous colonial overlords and nationalise the Suez Canal. The canal was the artery of empire, to the oil depots in Aden and the link to the East, not something we Europeans were going to easily relinquish. Full of the bravado of youth and completely sure that our cause was morally right and just, I was one of the paratroopers who were sent to liberate the Canal Zone and I jumped as part of that first wave over El Gamil Airfield.

We had boarded the plane in the early hours of an unusually warm November morning. I think it was a Dakota or a Valletta which had been stripped of any comforts and prepared as a transport. It was hot and stuffy, not helped by the fact we were carrying nearly our own body weight in equipment and rations. Everyone I was with seemed fired up with adrenaline, eager, fidgety and keen to get started rather than anxious or nervous about what lay ahead. It was a quick descent, which I must admit was quite scary. We were under fire from the Egyptian troops on the ground and helplessly dangling as a moving target is unnerving when there is nothing you can do but wait to hit the ground. We had flown in very low and with the weight of the Bren gun, ammunition, grenades and everything else it was only a short time before I felt the sand of the desert under my feet and was able to take cover behind an oil drum. We fought hard, as we were trained and in the blur of battle all around me, the details and precise sequence of events I can't exactly recall but I remember it was not long before we were successful in securing the airfield as was our mission objective. The whole show was soon over and before long I was back in Cyprus.

The politicians with their scheming machinations let us down, we were mere pawns in their global chess game. Why did they send us if we were not going to be able to finish the job properly? When I look back, I realise that I thought very differently then, I was younger, more naive and saw things from the perspective of a young soldier. People I knew were killed in that operation and at that time I was angry, it all seemed such a tragic waste.

I was in the army for only a very short time and I think after the Suez debacle I had had enough. The regiment came back to England the next year and I was demobbed. After that I decided on a complete change and went into a career in education. In the thirty years since then, I have had the time to reflect on what happened and what it really meant. Before Suez, Britain's place in the world was as a colonial power, we sat at the top table, we had clout, or so it seemed. I had grown up in a generation for whom that was the way of seeing the world and it was difficult to acknowledge the new order. I think of Suez as a fulcrum point, suddenly the weight shifted, the previous reality of Imperial power and influence and all the attitudes that went with that, no longer held true. My children are adults now but they are so different from all of my generation, they grew up with a very different perspective. Ten years ago my then teenage son came home one day sporting a tee shirt with an image of the Queen with a safety pin through her nose. I felt quite cross with him at first, a typical parent's response because I knew friends who had died for Queen and country, But when I thought about it I understood it was symptomatic of the new world view. Funnily enough five years later that same son was also fighting for Queen and country in the Falkland Islands. But that is another story.

The ward is buzzing with frantic activity as the morning comes. It doesn't begin to get light until after 7am and so much has to be done before then. There is a routine on the ward: patients should be awake, have had a cup of tea, made comfortable or turned before the day staff come in for report at 7:30. The "backs" have to all be done and there is a quota of patients to wash and get ready in order to save the day staff from having to do everything. This means turning on the lights at 6am, rudely waking everyone from sleep. I struggle to understand this. Our tutors in school have emphasised the importance of sleep as part of the healing process and yet here we are sounding the morning reveille. One might as well stand in the middle of the ward and play the trumpet at full volume. I remonstrate with the staff nurse but am given short shrift: the day staff have their own tasks to do and would complain if they had to do ours as well. "So much for patient-centred care" I mumble but get on with doing the jobs as asked. So often the ideals taught in nursing school come up against the realities of an understaffed system. Nursing is not always rewarding and sometimes it can be very frustrating as compromises need to be made. But I suppose that is a truth in any occupation.

7

DERBYSHIRE CHILDREN'S HOSPITAL

BIJAL'S STORY

Back on a surgical ward. I have escorted my patient to the anaesthetic room and am allowed to stay whilst the anaesthetist slowly administers the drug into the cannula on the back of the patient's hand. "I'd like you to count backwards from 10" he is saying as the syringe is depressed and the anaesthetic enters the blood stream. Vivek is looking up at the ceiling where there is a brightly-painted alphabet mural and doesn't get past eight as his eyes close. He gently succumbs to the desired effects of the medication looking peaceful as he falls into sleep. The very distressed crying and wailing that echoes from the walls, is coming from his mother, who is holding Vivek's other hand, unable to bear it as her 'baby' is prepared for his tonsillectomy. It's my job to lead her back through ward and to the day room, to try to comfort and reassure her as she waits for him to return and wake up for his jelly and ice cream.

Ward two at the Derbyshire Children's Hospital is a general surgical ward and also cares for children undergoing both ear nose and throat surgery and ophthalmic surgery. The hospital is a Victorian building, much smaller than either the Derby City hospital or the Derbyshire Royal Infirmary. Our placement here will include not only time on the ward but also some time spent in the various clinics held here. For some, children's nursing is a speciality they will choose after general training and at one time the Children's Hospital was the local centre where nurses could train solely as a children's nurse. It is not an aspect of nursing I'm looking forward to and I see the next two months as something that just needs to be got through.

Looking after sick children is not an easy job and not everyone is suited to it. I also think, that as my own children are both still very young it will be very difficult not to imagine oneself in the position of some of the parents who

43

accompany their offspring into the hospital, youngsters who could be in the hospital for anything from a routine correction of squint to treatment for a terminal illness.

I return to the day room with a cup of tea for Vivek's mother who seems much calmer now her son is not here. She is confident everything will go well, she believes the removal of Vivek's tonsils will stop the recurring sore throats and subsequent time away from school, but she just couldn't bear to watch as he slipped into medically induced unconsciousness. There are other patients to prepare for theatre and one of my jobs is to apply the soothing anaesthetic, which we call magic cream, to the backs of hands to numb the spot before a needle is inserted. Checking she is OK, I leave Bijal with her tea and go back into the ward.

These days it is common for children to go home after a tonsillectomy on the same day. Sometimes, if there is a lot of post-operative bleeding, a child may stay in overnight but back in 1988 it was a few days before the patient could go home. Vivek made a good recovery with no complications so two days later with his mother, he left the children's hospital and I carried on with the placement, looking forward to it finishing.

I met Bijal again a few years later. Being present whilst somebody has a difficult experience often means they have a vivid recollection of you. Bijal noticed me at a social event, whereas I did not recognise her at all. She came up to me, introduced herself and reminded me of that morning in the anaesthetic room. Strange the way friendships begin. We have now been friends for many years and over that time I have got to know some of her interesting history.

Bijal was born in Nairobi in Kenya in 1960 and has very fond memories of her early life in Africa. "We were quite privileged" she recalls. "My father owned a small printing business and life was really very good. Nairobi was a wonderful place, nice and warm all year round, and never too hot. We lived in a large house with such beautiful gardens. I expect it was because I was so small, but I can remember flowers and shrubs that towered over me, such colours and scents. Obviously I'm looking back through rose-coloured glasses but it was how you would imagine paradise. I was the youngest child and had two older brothers, and as the baby of the family I was utterly spoilt. We had an Ayah called Sahnib, she helped around the house and looked after us children. I know I was her favourite though, as she would sneak me newly baked savoury cup cakes from the kitchen." As such a small child, Bijal had no notion of the political climate and the way that after Kenyan independence attitudes had begun to change. One incident however is firmly fixed in her memory. "My eldest brother was beaten up on his way home from school. I remember him coming in with his face covered in blood, his eye swollen and closed and my mother screaming and crying. I can only have been about six or seven, but the horror of it is as vivid now as it was then. It turned out later that the fight was over a girl and nothing to do with what was happening to Asians in Kenya at the time, but I think it was in many ways the straw that broke my father's back."

It was shortly after this that Bijal and all her family left Kenya for good and came to Britain. Bijal did not fully understand the reasons for her uprooting and she found the change very traumatic. "We landed at Heathrow on a cold, rainy January morning. I followed my mother and brothers down the aircraft steps with my father behind us. I had no

45

coat and the cold rain began to soak through my clothes. I was utterly miserable but I don't really think I had any notion that this was now the rest of our lives. I also had no idea at the time that we only just made it here before the British government decided that our British passports would no longer allow us entry" The family had to leave much of what they owned in Kenya and start all over again in Britain. They made their way to Derby and began to rebuild their lives. Bijal's father opened a small corner shop and together working all the hours available the whole family gradually started the process of making a future.

"Those first few winters were the hardest" she tells me and recounts how she never got used to the cold winter mornings walking to school through snow. "I had seen snow" she said, " it sat on top of Mount Kilimanjaro looking beautiful under cloudless skies, but to walk on it, making your feet damp and cold, that was new and most unpleasant" I was quite surprised when I asked her about her experiences of racism. I had expected her to have many tales of intolerance and prejudice, but she said, "I really don't remember any obvious nasty incidents from my childhood but England was very different back in the 70's, attitudes weren't the same then and we tolerated things that thankfully just wouldn't be acceptable now" The family settled into the local Gujarati community active in the Hindu temple, and gradually memories of halcyon days with all-year-round sunshine faded under grey midlands clouds.

Bijal is a grandmother now. Vivek, that little boy on Ward two at the children's hospital is now a grown man with children of his own. The Victorian building on North street has long gone, demolished and replaced with housing. The children's hospital is now part of a new modern sprawling mega hospital, the Derby Royal which has gradually spread out from its roots as the Derby City Hospital. Bijal's father and mother are both now dead and never returned to Kenya before they passed away. "What about you" I once asked Bijal, "would you go back?" She gave my question a few minutes thought before she replied. "No, England is my home, most of my life I have been here. My children and grandchildren were born here, it is our home". And then after a few more minutes in a whimsical voice, she added, "Perhaps a safari holiday might be nice though, a chance to see the equatorial sun once more and maybe find out what became of my Ayah, but then maybe not, some things are better left where they are."

I was actually quite sorry to finish at the children's hospital. For all my reticence about working there, I actually found the experience very rewarding. I would not choose to specialise as a children's nurse, as for me the line between compassion and distance would all too easily be crossed and I would not cope well with the ongoing emotional trauma. I am however glad that I had the experience as part of my general nurse training and especially to have been fortunate to be able to undertake the allocation at Derby's dedicated children's hospital. It was a small friendly environment with everybody knowing everybody else, a special place that was not part of a bigger impersonal hospital building. It was a place with a history, years of caring for children at their most vulnerable etched into the Victorian fabric of the building. There may be a logic to rationalising resources and locating all services in one mega institution, to build a new and up-to-date facility where everything is on hand. There will be economies of scale, access to the latest facilities, the best in medical and surgical care all immediately available without having to shuffle to a different hospital for a scan or specific consultation. It could be argued that these are changes bound to improve on the clinical outcomes for the patients and yet something was lost when the children's hospital closed and everything moved to the new Derby Royal. Something not readily tangible, something not measurable on a spreadsheet, something not easily identified, but lost nevertheless.

8

KINGSWAY PSYCHIATRIC HOSPITAL

ANN-MARIE'S STORY

We are walking on a winding pathway across an expanse of verdant green grass, heading towards a red brick building in the distance, chatting nervously to each other, hoping to disguise the trepidation we are all feeling. Suddenly a pair of double doors swings open and a small, insignificant-looking figure hurtles through them, over a little paved area and on to the grass, heading straight towards us at an alarming rate of knots. Almost immediately he is followed by a larger-looking man who dives forward and rugby tackles the first person down to the ground. Within seconds there are two others at the scene and the absconder is returned through the double doors which close behind them, the little drama over. I almost expect them all to return to this improvised stage and take a small bow, which of course they don't.

Myself and two other students are on our way to the acute admissions unit at Kingsway Hospital, one of Derby's two large psychiatric hospitals, for an afternoon's orientation visit prior to beginning a nine week allocation. The tableau we have just witnessed does little to alleviate our increasing anxiety.

Although we are general nursing students, we have been making use of the psychiatric students' educational facilities at the other psychiatric hospital, Pastures, before staring our placement on the psychiatric ward. This morning's lecture was the last of these sessions and tried to cover the huge topic of "what is normal?" a question to which I still do not know the answer. Our classroom lessons are now finished and after our brief visit later today, we will begin this next important practical part of the training. Treatment on a general ward for a physical health problem does not preclude somebody from also suffering from a mental health problem, and these next few weeks are an essential part of a nurse's holistic education. Knowing this does not stop me from feeling unsure and worried about what to expect. Other than the last few weeks of lectures, my only knowledge of a psychiatric ward has been shaped by seeing the menacing Nurse Ratchet in "One Flew Over the Cuckoo's Nest", and a wonderful BBC TV series called "Maybury" which starred Patrick Stewart as a hospital psychiatrist.

Working at Kingsway is vastly different experience from any of my previous nursing and the first major difficulty was to establish who were the staff and who were the patients. Bill is a staff nurse, he must be because he has just introduced himself as such but initially I'm not completely sure as we have just witnessed him showing his skills as a scrum- half. He takes us round the unit, showing us various areas and presenting us to staff and patients and tells us he is looking forward to seeing us again on the following Monday morning when we begin our first shift.

After a few weeks of working at Kingsway, (I say working but we are mostly here in a supernumerary capacity, to watch and learn) I find that I am starting to become familiar with the environment. We are encouraged to read through patients' notes, to learn something of the different psychiatric diagnoses, and relate these to the symptoms we observe with the patients. Although we could read the notes, patients themselves were not permitted to do so as this was a time before people had legal access to the Holy of Holies and could see what had been written about them on their medical records. This state of affairs explains some of the terms used by doctors, that would not be used today. I came across a few abbreviations that I had not seen before and asked one of the junior doctors to explain what they meant. Following a long description of some strange and bizarre symptoms, one doctor had written in large capitals, "GOK". I was attempting to work out what it could possibly refer to, "Generalised Obsessive Kleptomania" perhaps or "Gradual Occasional Kalemia"? I am told in an almost weary tone, "it's what we put when we have no idea, it just means God Only Knows". Psychiatry, it would seem, could sometimes be a lot less precise than general medicine.

General nursing students were often called upon to perform tasks that were seen to be within our remit, taking a blood pressure or giving an injection for example. George was prescribed his antipsychotic drug as depot injection, a slow release version of his medication which was administered every four weeks, an obvious job for the general student who would be completely confident and experienced with such a procedure. Suspended in an oily substance, a depot injection requires a large needle and a determined push to get all the way in. George is not bothered, he drops his trousers and leans over the couch in the clinical room and presents a suitable muscle for the needle. "A sharp scratch," say I, and using a z-tracking technique the point goes in, slightly withdrawn to ensure a blood vessel has not been compromised, then the medication is slowly administered as the plunger is depressed. By this stage of our training, I have given many, many injections, I am practised, confident and comfortable in the environment of the clinical room. I have however never experienced the thick, viscous oily substance I am trying to get into George's backside, into a muscle which at that very moment George tenses up to create an impenetrable barrier. Feeling the unexpected resistance I push harder. Something has to give and it does, the needle detaches from the syringe and the oily slime explodes all over me, George and every available surface in the clinical room, including Bill. His only response is a sarcastic "Done many injections have you?"

The Psychiatric ward is a clinical environment where taking time to talk to the patients and get to know them is positively encouraged rather than being just a brief moment or two snatched between a never ending list of tasks. Ann-Marie was somebody whom I got to know and hers was a tragic story.

Ann-Marie was a troubled young single mother and had a long history of mental health problems. She had been taken under the wing of a caring couple from a local church. They had genuine compassion for Ann-Marie and endeavoured not only to be a spiritual support but also to help out in practical ways, babysitting for Kimberly, her 18-month-old baby, and Michele, her three-year-old toddler, and also providing the occasional gifts of groceries and clothing. Ann-Marie became an enthusiastic member of the church fellowship and in many ways her past difficulties seemed to be gradually getting better and better. But the shadow of psychosis hung over Ann-Marie like a sword of Damocles, her state of good mental health always balanced on a knife edge. Sure enough, Ann-Marie began to become ill again. It was unlikely to have been postpartum psychosis, triggered by the birth of Kimberly, she was now over a year old, but more likely the recurrence of a long-standing illness. Ann-Marie started thinking strange thoughts, believing strange ideas and her experience of being in a lively church began to filter into her delusions. She started to hear voices and believed herself to be possessed by the Devil. The church desperately wanted to help poor Ann-Marie but struggled, as although Ann-Marie's mental health history was known to them, they perceived what was happening to her as a spiritual attack and tried to cast out what they believed to be very real manifestations of evil. This heady, frantic atmosphere of attempted exorcism and fervent prayer only seemed to send Ann-Marie further and further into her state of delusion, her grip on reality becoming less secure with each passing day. The church members gradually realised that Ann-Marie was severely ill and called the GP and eventually she was sectioned under the mental health act and admitted to our ward for 28 days to be assessed.

Ann-Marie was a young women with a childlike, sweet voice who could communicate with you as though everything was completely normal. She would talk of the weather or how grateful she was to the couple from church who cared for her and then halfway through whatever she was saying, she would stop and seeing the attentive expression on her face, you knew she was hearing a voice, her previous conversation with you now completely forgotten. When someone is utterly convinced that they are controlled by a malevolent spirit, they can be quite scary to be around, a bit like finding yourself in the film "The Exorcist". Ann-Marie could change her voice to a deep and menacing growl and speak as though she was the evil she believed was in her head.

The antipsychotic drugs began to have an effect, the auditory and visual hallucinations that bombarded her became less and less and it was decided after her time in hospital she was well enough to be entrusted to the care of friends. Reunited with Kimberly and Michele, Ann-Marie seemed happy and very glad to be out of Kingsway. I think she felt a connection with me and she promised to write to me and keep in contact and I agreed she could. I was a young and inexperienced student and unwisely did not seek advice from the psychiatric nurses as to whether letting her have my address was a good idea. However after she had left the ward, I thought it would be the last I saw of Ann-

Marie.

It was months later that I found out what happened to Ann-Marie. Her psychotic symptoms began to reoccur, perhaps because when she felt well, she did not think she needed to take her medication. The dark voices returned, with a terrible command, they told her Kimberly was a manifestation of evil, her baby was a danger to her and she needed to rid herself of the problem. She was very open and honest to the couple she was staying with, but her matter of fact tone belied the real intent. They prayed with her, reassured her she was getting better and said goodnight, leaving Ann-Marie and Kimberly alone in their room and Michele asleep in her own room. That night Ann-Marie calmly took a pillow and gently suffocated the life out of her youngest daughter, then went to the room of the couple and told them what she had done.

I read about it in the local paper and although I found it awfully upsetting, I was not entirely surprised. Her altered thoughts, which could have been a simple chemical imbalance or maybe even a demon with horns and a pitchfork, had won.

Ann-Marie did write, I had my first letter from her, sent from the remand wing of a women's prison, some distance from Derby. She was remorseful, the enormity of what had happened difficult for her to accept and she was requesting if I would please go and visit. I saw her twice whilst she was on remand, her gentle, sweet voice talking about prison food, how the prison hospital was very like Kingsway and then suddenly, mid conversation, she would stop, just like before, a far away look on her face as the voices filled her head.

After her trial, Ann-Marie was sent to a secure hospital to be detained "at her Majesty's pleasure". She only wrote to me from there once and then her letters just stopped. After all this time I do not know if she is still there or whether she has been successfully treated and is now well, living a happy and productive life. But I do wonder if the tragedy of Ann-Marie was something that could have been prevented, whether the system, her friends or I, had in someway failed her.

The places of asylum which back then represented the way in which mental health problems were treated, have long since gone. Replaced by care in the community, mental illness is supposed to be no longer locked away out of sight and out of mind. But to adequately care for patients in the community, is not a cheap option. If done well it requires a far larger amount of resources than the old psychiatric hospitals ever did. And like a lot of good ideas on paper, the reality often doesn't meet the expectations. Vulnerable people have on too many occasions been inadequately supported, left to fend for themselves, hard-pressed community nurses struggling to cope. And what of the asylum, the place of safety? Too few beds available for those in desperate need who sometimes have to travel hundreds of miles to find a place. Maybe in the eagerness to reform and do away with the long stay wards where patients sometimes became institutionalised, something was lost. The time that I spent on the acute admissions ward at Kingsway Hospital was just a short part of my overall training. It was just a brief couple of months, an intense and at times harrowing departure from the hustle and bustle of general nursing. There wasn't the time to cover the many other aspects of psychiatric care such as working in the community or to see those now-closed long stay wards and so I just had this brief glimpse of one particular aspect of the discipline. It was however a very informative and interesting glimpse which is an essential part of general nurses training.

Dave Eldergill

9

WARD 11, ORTHOPAEDICS, DERBYSHIRE ROYAL INFIRMARY

JOHN'S STORY

Sister Smith is standing next to me and watching every move with eagle eyes. John has a deep wound on his left thigh and my job is to clean and redress the wound using an aseptic technique. It is a well-defined procedure, with a correct method of opening the sterile pack, of moving soiled dressings and not crossing the sterile field and every aspect of the procedure is scrutinised by Sister Smith's watchful eye. John also observes every move, as though detached from his own limb. He has a very quirky sense of humour and as I clean with sterile saline I am wondering the wisdom of picking John's gradually healing leg for this important clinical assessment. He could easily decide to do something just for the fun of it, that could mean the whole test having to be done again. Fortunately for me he is, on this occasion, the perfect, compliant patient and I pass with flying colours. John is one of a number of patients who are much younger than most of those I have nursed up until now. This because I have now begun a new allocation, working on ward eleven at the Derbyshire Royal Infirmary, male orthopaedic. This is where young, daredevil motorcyclists come to be put back together, when as in Johns case they have an argument with a stationary tree.

Our time in the school of nursing prior to starting on the ward, has been spent becoming familiar with the musculoskeletal system, trying to remember all those Latin names of bones, muscles and tendons and learning that the terminology used in the song "Dem Dry Bones" is not necessarily anatomically accurate. Whilst on the ward I encounter a whole range of new nursing experiences. Elective surgery to replace tired knees and worn-out hips, emergency surgery to mend broken bones with all manner of what look like Heath Robinson constructions with pulleys, levers and weights. Experimental procedures to reattach severed appendages using live leeches to stimulate blood flow, and delicate, intricate surgery to hands or feet. Many patients are confined to bed with ropes and pulleys holding immobilised limbs in traction.

It may be hard to believe now, but patients unable to leave their beds were allowed to smoke on the ward. Glowing cigarette ends were perilously close to piped oxygen on the wall. Some things were very different in the 1980s! Other patients are on the way back to mobility with a steadily increasing speed on crutches or wheelchairs. Apart from the results of their injuries, this ward seems to be full of otherwise fit and healthy but often very bored young men.

John had been admitted to hospital from casualty after a road traffic accident. He had swerved to avoid a car which had turned right, straight into his path, oblivious of his oncoming motorcycle. Swerving and accelerating to get out of trouble he managed to avoid the car, but couldn't avoid ploughing into a large, ancient and immovable oak tree and was thrown from his bike. The car driver at this point noticed him and stopped to help, constantly apologising with the refrain familiar to all motorbike riders "Sorry mate, I didn't see you". The severity of John's injuries required immediate surgical intervention and he came to ward eleven from casualty via the orthopaedic operating theatre. Some bones had been fixed with external bars, pins protruding from his iodine-soaked flesh. Others had been reduced and immobilised in plaster and others held apart with traction. John was going to be on the ward for quite a while.
Strangely, John had very few family visitors and whilst his bones slowly began to knit back together, I learned a little about why that was.

John came from a small mining town in the North of the county, and like his father before him, he and his brother had left school to work in the local pit. Mining was hard and dirty work but the coal mine was the only major local employer. The community had grown around the mine, the community was the mine. John had married his girlfriend Debbie in 1980, they had been together since they were at school but his older brother Jim was much more of a "Jack the lad" and was showing no signs of settling down. By 1984 John was a father of two children, had a mortgage on a little two-up-two-down terraced house and was studying maths at night school. He didn't want to spend the next 30 years underground and hoped eventually to train as a bookkeeper. Jim on the other hand was still relishing the single life, with a succession of girlfriends, one after the other which he would bring to his brother's house of an evening and promptly forget their names whilst introducing them to the stable and reliable side of the family. The brothers were like chalk and cheese, but still really enjoyed each others' company, both sharing an overwhelming passion for Nottingham Forest football team which Jim seemed to be able to go and see play, far more often than John.

In March of 1984 the mineworkers went on strike, determined to stand up and fight against a Conservative government equally determined to force the closure of many pits and to destroy the power of the National Union of Mineworkers. All the family members who worked at the mine joined the strike: both brothers, their father who was a union official, and two uncles. There was a sense of camaraderie, of being in it together and through terrible hardship, the community endured. Neither John or Jim could not afford to see their beloved football team any more when there was barely enough money to feed the children, but everyone rallied round and supported each other. Debbie and the children received a measly £11 a week in supplementary benefit and the union did not have the funds to issue strike pay, even though its equivalent amount was being deducted from the benefit that should have been given. The family only managed to eat because of a communal kitchen set up by all the wives and supplied with generous donations from many sympathetic friends. Bills though, including the mortgage, didn't get paid, and the pressure of mounting debt began to take its toll on the family.

After eight months, with an approaching winter, John began to buckle under the strain. There were constant arguments with Debbie over money and the house was getting colder and colder with nothing left to burn on the fire. John began to question the wisdom of the strike. He started to view the union leader, Arthur Scargill as the enemy rather than just the Prime Minister, Margaret Thatcher. Was his family's suffering the result of the political ambitions of an embittered union leader who had chosen not to call a national ballot? John felt like an expendable pawn in somebody else's game. It seemed as though he and his family were going to be collateral damage in a fight between a Prime Minister bent on revenge over a previous strike that had brought down a government, and a union determined to hold on and fight for what they believed was right, at no matter what cost. The simple black and white, us and them, equations no longer seemed to add up so John made a momentous decision. He would join the breakaway Union of Democratic Mineworkers, and go back to work.

A steady trickle of miners had returned to work, the quantity increasing by a few more each week and John became one of their number, crossing the picket line manned by members of his own family. The first that Jim knew of what he thought of as his brother's treachery, was when he saw John's face looking back at him from the bus window as it sped through the angry shouts of "scab" hurled by the massed pickets at the colliery gate.

There was a bitter confrontation between the brothers after John's shift had finished and that was then followed by a cold silence. Nobody spoke to John or Debbie, they became "*personae non grata,*" ostracised and outside the embrace of family. John would occasionally meet his mother in the park with his children, a grandmother desperate to see her growing grandchildren, but their conversations were strained. Her anguish at his betrayal and her loyalty to her husband robbing her of any joy in watching her grandchildren play.

The following March, nearly a year after it had begun, the strike ended and the miners returned to work. John had left the pit by then and started a new career as manager of a supermarket. He had moved with Debbie and the children to Nottingham, the few miles' physical distance emphasising the chasm that existed between him and the rest of his family. John didn't see himself as a traitor to his roots and thought the perception of him as a scab was unfair. He believed he was questioning the validity and wisdom of the strike and felt that the crushing defeat and destruction of the coal industry was as much the fault of the union as it was of the government. Nobody else in his extended family saw it that way and the family remained fractured.

One evening during visiting time, I noticed a grey-haired lady, in her sixties, sat next to John's bed, deep in conversation with him. Later, as I was going from patient to patient, taking the regular observations, checking limbs for sensation and circulation, asking about pain relief and the myriad of other important tasks that have the effect of making a patient less of an individual and more a job to be done, I asked John about his visitor. "That was my mother" he answered. He went on to tell me he was hopeful that it may be possible for a family reconciliation. His mother had been told of his accident and wanted to come and see him, and even his father, when hearing of his hospitalisation, had shown signs of softening. "And your brother?" I asked. "Who knows?" he said, "who knows?"

The next day on an early shift, sitting in Sister Smith's office waiting for morning report, I looked up the ward and noticed John's bed was empty. Nothing unusual in that, bed moves were common. Shifting patients into side rooms, making space for new admissions to be near to the office was something that was done all the time. Everybody carried on chatting and I was ready with my scrap of paper, prepared to make notes using some newly acquired orthopaedic shorthand, # for fracture, THR, total hip replacement and many others that were slowly becoming familiar. I was aware that the night sister was looking visibly upset as she came into the office and sat down ready to hand over the ward. John, she informed everyone with a shaky voice, had died in the night. She went on to explain that he had suffered from a fat embolus, a rare but potential complication following long bone fractures, most often occurring in the first two days after injury but sometimes, as in John's case, up to two weeks after the event. In effect, a small globule of fat, loose in the blood stream had caused a blockage in his lungs and caused rapid death. Everybody in the office was stunned. Deaths on ward eleven were rare and if we are honest, John's young age, similar to most of us who worked on the ward, was a salient reminder of our own mortality. It was hard to comprehend that this young vibrant, funny individual, to all intents and purposes making a good recovery following such a horrendous motorbike crash, was suddenly no more.

I don't know the conclusion to John's family's story. He was gone, and the routine of the orthopaedic ward had to carry on as before. We only see up to a certain point and then the story continues without us, our part in its telling being finished. It remains unknown to me if Debbie and the two young children were alone at the funeral. Did the family rally round, let the past remain in the past and be the support the grieving widow needed? Those answers I don't know but I do know that within a few years the pit had closed anyway, the community was left devastated and divided and a former proud industry had been destroyed. Working down a mine is an awful, dangerous occupation. I have nursed many former miners with long-term lung damage caused by years down the pit. If, as a society we can find sustainable and more ecologically beneficial ways of meeting our energy needs, so that men don't have to spend their days labouring in the dark underground then that has to be better. But to effect that change by ripping the heart out of communities, by setting brother against brother, father against son and to make no effort to replace the lost jobs and incomes, is a callous and cynical act and not one motivated by a genuine desire to make the world a better place.

Dave Eldergill

10

ACCIDENT AND EMERGENCY,
DERBYSHIRE ROYAL INFIRMARY

MAJAX

Male nurses constitute roughly 10% of registered nurses in the United Kingdom. In speciality areas such as critical care or accident and emergency, the proportion is significantly higher. Perhaps it is the perceived excitement and flow of adrenaline that attracts male nurses to these areas but for me as a male student nurse, about to begin an allocation in the casualty department of the Derbyshire Royal Infirmary, excitement was a notion that seemed considerably overrated.

Each new group of students begins their time in the department strictly supervised by trained and experienced staff. We sit in and watch as lacerations are stitched together and simple fractures reduced. We are allowed to observe from the sidelines as major injuries and accidents are brought into the crash room, and as confidence increases we are gradually given more and more things to do. Some of those things were more difficult and worrying than others.

I am asked to accompany a patient to X-Ray as he has just had a distal forearm fracture manipulated using a Bier's block anaesthetic. This is where a tourniquet is applied to the upper arm using an inflatable cuff enabling the anaesthetic to be just kept in the limb. I'm given stern warnings by the staff nurse about making sure the cuff does not deflate as the porter wheels us down to the X-ray because if it does the resulting rush of lignocaine into the rest of the body could anaesthetise the patients heart muscle. The junior doctor who has just reduced the patient's Colles' fracture seems rather blasé about this potential complication whereas I am struggling not to let my nervousness upset the patient or worse still, not to let the anxious shake of my hand cause the very thing I am worried about.

Our time is split between the acute admissions area and the follow up and minor procedure clinics, known for some reason in Derby as "the back row". Here I assist as stitches are removed and I learn useful new techniques such as how to tie a sling or remove a plaster cast using a plaster saw. (Not as awful as it sounds as the saw blade only vibrates and does not spin and therefore can't cut the skin) I am particularly impressed to see a finger trephine performed. A builder had missed the end of a masonry nail with his hammer and unfortunately made painful contact with the end of his finger. An X-ray had revealed nothing was broken but a large and very painful blood blister had formed under the fingernail. To get rid of the pain from the increased pressure that this subungual haematoma is causing, the staff nurse I am assisting uses a state-of-the-art piece of surgical technology. Unfolding a paperclip she heats the end in a flame until it glows red hot. This is then placed on the affected digit and gently pushed through the nail. Immediately dark congealing blood spurts and then oozes out, releasing the build-up of pressure thereby giving immediate relief from the pain. The overwhelming aroma of burning flesh is a little disconcerting though.

Gender stereotypes seem to be learned at a very young age. A five-year-old boy had been brought to casualty by his very distressed mother after an injury to the head. Head wounds, even when superficial, can bleed profusely and I am attempting to comfort the mother and help a young female junior doctor glue together what has luckily turned out to be only a small cut. The little boy is unable to grasp that I am the nurse and the lady in the white coat is the doctor. Fortunately, however, this contradiction to his world view is a convenient distraction as his head is stuck back together.

It was during my allocation in Derby's Accident and Emergency Department that I was able to witness the magnificent way the NHS responds to a major crisis. On the evening of January 8th 1989 a British Midland Boeing 737 crashlanded at East Midlands airport after impacting with the embankment of the M1 motorway and leaping over the fortunately empty carriageway. I had been working that day on an early shift and was relaxing watching television at home in Derby when I heard what had happened on a newsflash. I initially thought the report was to do with the Lockerbie air disaster, as that had occurred only a few weeks before, but as I watched I realised this was something new and very close to Derby. Local hospitals in Derby, Nottingham and Leicester had put into operation their major accident procedures. These are policies put in place to cope with an incident such as this. It would be nice to be able to recount a story of how I was a hero, called back to work to put my not-so-many years of experience into practice, saving traumatised lives. What actually happened was that I telephoned the hospital and was told that sufficient trained and experienced staff had gone back to the department and to an emptied orthopaedic ward ready to receive casualties. Where I would really be needed was the next day when it would be necessary for extra staff to go on shift and let the teams working overnight go home and rest.

My experience of that momentous event is that of the 'morning after the night before' when there was an eerie quietness in the emergency department. The casualties had already been brought in by ambulance, triaged to prioritise clinical needs, treated and sent on to operating theatres and wards. The next morning on my shift, I and other colleagues took over from the exhausted night staff, the maelstrom of activity now over. Television crews were still camped outside and there did not seem to be any genuine patients about at all but only voyeurs and reporters sniffing around for a story, complaining of trivial ailments to get access to the department and find out what had happened the night before.

In the 1980s, air travel was, and still is to this day, statistically the safest form of travel. The passengers and crew aboard the British Midland flight 92 from London Heathrow to Belfast on the evening of January 8th 1989 would have known this, but would also have been aware of the fact that only eighteen days previously, a Boeing 747 flying to America from Frankfurt via London had been tragically and cruelly destroyed by a terrorist bomb. Blown from the sky over Scotland, killing all 259 people on board and also a further 11 people on the ground in Lockerbie, where the wreckage of the plane impacted with the earth and burst into searing flame. A terrible and awful loss of life caused not by accident but by a wilful and deliberate act of callous inhumanity. That devastating event would no doubt have been in the minds of the passengers as they climbed the stairs and boarded the plane, perhaps increasing the anxiety felt as their flight accelerated along the runway and lifted off the ground and into the sky. Maybe hands were squeezed and heart rates increased more than usual on that routine takeoff but everything was normal, and the Boeing 737 began climbing to reach its cruising altitude of 35,000 feet. Whilst still climbing and at about 28,300 feet, a blade detached from the fan of the left engine. The passengers would have heard the noise, would have felt the vibrations, been aware of a burning smell and seen smoke coming into the cabin from the ventilation system. Some of the passengers at the rear of the plane looking out of the windows also noticed smoke and sparks coming from the left engine. A slowly rising terror would have been rationalised, there must be a reasonable explanation, everything will be ok, if there is problem with one engine then we can land with the other.

The plane was diverted, it could land at East Midlands airport using the remaining engine, so not a major crisis but just an inconvenience for everyone, but safety comes first. What happened next has been scrutinised and investigated and many lessons have been learned so hopefully it will never happen again. The pilots mistakenly believed that the right-sided engine was the problem and shut it down and as the plane approached East Midlands, they pumped more fuel into the damaged engine in an attempt to maintain speed. This unfortunately had the effect of causing the already damaged engine to burst into flames and cease to function at all. A last minute attempt was made to restart the one remaining good engine, but by the now the aircraft was travelling too slowly for this to work. The tail hit the ground just before the M1 motorway and flipped the plane back into the air and over the road, breaking into three parts just before the runway of East Midlands Airport. As events unfolded, right up until impact, were the passengers and crew suppressing their fear? Not really believing it was happening? Sure at some level that all was under control and everything would be all right?

There were 118 passengers and eight members of crew on board flight 92. 39 of those passengers died in the crash and a further eight did not survive their injuries. All eight members of the crew survived. 50 of the survivors, most with serious life-threatening injuries were taken to the A&E department of the Derbyshire Royal Infirmary where experienced staff worked tirelessly throughout the night to treat the traumatised victims and the horrendous injuries with which they were confronted.

Later the next day, as is the way with politicians, whether to boost their own popularity or, as one would like to think, because they believe it might do some actual good, Margaret Thatcher, the Prime Minister at the time, and an accompanying entourage came to visit the Royal Infirmary to meet and shake hands with some of the staff involved. During her tour of the department the normal routine of admissions and patients' treatment had to continue as usual. I was on an early shift and was sent with another student into the Crash Room to assist with a seriously ill patient who had just been brought in via ambulance. We were "gofers", running about to get needles, syringes, and all manner of pipes and tubes requested by the doctor and staff nurse who were treating the unfortunate casualty. Monitors were attached, drugs pushed in and the initial rush of activity subsided as the patient's condition was stabilised. It was then that both the doctor and staff nurse were called away, as it was their turn to "press the flesh" of the visiting dignitaries. We had our instructions: check the monitors, watch for signs of a deteriorating condition, call for help if we needed it. Suddenly the room filled with the sound of unexplained beeps and alarms. The monitor had a strange pattern neither of us students had seen before and our patient's lips seemed to be turning a funny shade of blue which our nearly two years of training told us was not normal. We called for help but nobody came and it seemed to us that the patient was deciding to shuffle off his mortal coil. In a moment of crisis, time seems to dig in its heels and slow right down. In reality, very quickly the room was full of practiced, skilled clinicians responding to the situation and ensuring the survival of the prostrate form lying on the bed. But to me, it was an eternity of helplessness, I was scared and not qualified to administer the necessary drugs, intubation tube or anything else whilst waiting for those who were, to return back to duty. The lack of resources in this critical moment, were a direct result of a politician's actions. What a metaphor for health care in general.

11

ORTHOPAEDIC THEATRE, DERBYSHIRE ROYAL INFIRMARY

SISTER WINTER

Maurice is about to undergo an operation for a Charnley Total Hip Replacement. He is wide awake and has been chatting with the anaesthetist. A green surgical drape blocks Maurice's potential view of the procedure that is to be performed and soothing music is pumped through headphones which the anaesthetist is placing over his ears. "Try to relax" he tells him as he carefully puts them into position on Maurice's head. He continues to monitor Maurice's vital signs and the levels of the spinal anaesthetic he has given him. Today is my second day of an operating theatre allocation. I am assigned to the orthopaedic theatres and have been allowed into theatre number two to observe my first operation. I am dressed in surgical scrubs, which back in 1989 were reserved for use in theatres and not worn by all hospital staff as is today's norm. We change into the freshly-laundered clothes as we enter and leave them there to be washed again as we depart. It feels as though I am now in the holy sanctum, dressed in the robes of the acolyte and am about to witness my first sacred ritual. This is how it seems to me, but to the initiated it is just another day in the operating theatre.

The very name, operating theatre, conjures up the idea of spectacle, a place of high drama, a surgical performance. Traditionally it would have been a tiered amphitheatre in which students and other spectators could watch the speed with which a skilled surgeon could remove a limb from a conscious patient. In a time before anaesthetic, speed and accuracy counted for more than a university doctorate. These deft moves with knife and saw were tasks performed by apprenticeship-trained barber surgeons and not by the academically trained physicians. Even now, in a kind of reverse snobbery, surgeons use the title "Mr" rather than "Dr". In some teaching hospitals today, a screened gallery still exists so that students can observe and learn from more senior staff. We, however, are allowed to see what is happening from inside the room, told to keep back and keep quiet, to watch and learn.

The orthopaedic surgeon has to dislocate Maurice's hip, which involves putting the leg into a most unnatural position. Maurice looks up and is confronted by his own leg, seemingly the wrong way round yet he recognises his own foot. He feels no sensation, the anaesthetic having completely numbed his lower half, but he is nevertheless disconcerted by the surprising appearance of his own leg in this unexpected location. The anaesthetist lifts away the headphones and reassures Maurice that everything is ok, and the foot disappears from Maurice's sight.

The headphones are placed back over Maurice's ears and the sounds of drills, electric saws and hammers are obscured by the very loud voice of Luciano Pavarotti's rendition of "Nessun Dorma". It is fascinating to see, and luckily I am not at all squeamish at the sight of skin and muscle being cut apart and bone being sawn off. It is, after all, not my leg!

The theatre suite is a closed world, and to leave it to go to the hospital canteen would require changing out of the theatre scrubs, so tea breaks and lunches are generally taken in the small staff room within the suite. Everyone soon gets to know everyone else and even nursing students like me, who are only staying for a brief nine-week allocation, are soon chatting with other members of staff, the social interaction helping to foster a sense of being part of the team. Sister Winter is in charge of the orthopaedic theatres. She runs a tight ship and even the most arrogant of consultant surgeons acknowledge and defer to her position in the hierarchy. I like talking to Sister Winter. She is twenty years older than me but somehow we manage to make a connection. I do however find her broad Glaswegian accent a little intimidating. I asked her on one occasion if she missed the interactions with awake patients that she had when working on wards. She looked at me with a haughty expression and replied "my dear boy..." (I was a lot younger then but the term was one of superiority, not endearment or affection) "...I came to theatre to get away from awake patients". Contrary to the accepted wisdom in orthopaedic theatres, Sister Winter was not the stern, scary figure she at first seemed and the putatively fierce persona was just an affectation which hid a genuinely caring nature.

Edith Winter didn't begin her nursing career until she was 35, having been, up until then, a high-flyer working in a Scottish bank. She had determined that if anyone could break through the glass ceiling, she could, and as such she gave everything to her career. Marriage and children could wait, her work became her whole life. She did well. Along with her drive, work ethic and natural talent she was also a well-liked member of staff who would always be willing to help a colleague when needed. And so throughout her twenties, she gradually climbed the corporate ladder, moving from being everyone's favourite employee to becoming everyone's favourite boss. This was the way her life would have progressed until fate capriciously decided to throw her a wild card.

It was what she described as a "near-death experience" that caused her to revaluate everything and put her on the path she now follows. "I'd had a headache for about a week but kept it just about at bay with regular paracetamol. Work was busy and it just seemed the stress of the job was taking its toll. Early on a crisp autumnal Tuesday morning in September, I was just about to leave for work. I liked to be one step ahead of the rush hour traffic. As I got into the car

I felt a horrendous pain in the side of my head, I can only describe it as like being hit very hard with a blunt object. Everything after that is all very hazy, I know I fell to the floor and a passer-by telephoned 999, but these are facts I only found out at a later date". Sister Winter looked almost embarrassed as she recounted the details of the next part of her story, as though she didn't believe them herself but needed the reassurance that what she experienced was not completely absurd. "I had in that time what seemed like a strange but very realistic dream. I was looking down at myself, lying on a trolley in casualty and seeing doctors and nurses running around putting in tubes and attaching wires. I was very aware that it was me and yet not me lying below. That I could be in one place seeing myself in another didn't feel weird but normal. I know this sounds cliched," she says in an almost apologetic tone, "but I saw a bright light in the corner of the room and I felt drawn towards it, it was as though a gradually increasing visual sense of peace and love was calling me. I next remember coming round in the recovery room, the bright light was made of plastic and I was being gently roused by the nurse. I had this overwhelming feeling of disappointment! It was later explained to me that I had had a subarachnoid haemorrhage, a blood vessel ruptured and bled inside my skull and that my life had been very much in the balance. I had been extremely fortunate, a quick witted commuter, trained in first aid had been on the scene almost immediately. The rapid response of the ambulance, skill of the team in the neurological theatres and dedicated post operative care and physiotherapy ensured not only my survival but also that I made a full recovery. I now know all the theories about the brain's responses to diminished oxygen, how common these experiences are, but I have never been able to shake off the memory of that feeling of floating above my body and the very real desire to move

towards the light."
"So deciding to train as a nurse was a way of giving
something back after your excellent treatment?" I had asked
her.
"Well yes" she had replied "but not just that, I had a
different perspective on what was important, I wanted to
do something that I thought really mattered and here I am
more than decade on making sure that the patients who
come through my theatre suite, receive the same high
standard of care as I did".

Sister Winter was a dedicated nurse, but she often would
say how difficult it was to maintain her high standards in
the male-centric, macho surroundings of orthopaedic
theatre. Perhaps it was the preponderance of power tools,
the undeniable egos of the mostly male orthopaedic
surgeons and the closed-in hermetically sealed environment
which sometimes allowed for the atmosphere and banter of
a garage workshop to prevail.

One of the roles of a nurse is to be a patient's advocate, to
help to maintain someone's individuality against a medical
model which so often sees a person merely in terms of the
illness they present with. My time in theatre and the
example of nurses of the calibre of Sister Winter, helped to
draw this aspect of nursing into sharp focus. I can
remember on one occasion, early on during my time in
theatre when again as new inexperienced students our role
was only to observe, I witnessed Sister Winter at her
patient's representative best. A young woman was being
prepared to have a series of plates and screws attached to
fix a badly damaged ankle. A young orthopaedic registrar,
and two male operating department assistants were moving
the affected limb into position ready to operate. Scant
regard was given to the personal dignity of the unaware

patient as her flimsy, paper operating gown did little to protect her modesty. Sister Winter who had been preparing the instrument tray, turned around to see this manoeuvre in progress as the three men discussed the previous weekend's football scores, seemingly oblivious and unconcerned by the undignified naked flesh on full display. A Glaswegian accent, when projected angrily across a small space is enough to make the most macho man quiver and her reprimand soon had its desired effect. Nobody was going to forget that this was a person under her care and not a mere slab of meat on which to practise organic meccano.

Theatre was overall a rewarding time. We had day trips to the hospital's other theatres to watch a variety of general surgery, ear, nose and throat surgery and even some very delicate procedures on eyes. We learned the role of the nurse in the anaesthetic room, the circulating nurse and scrub nurse. We were told of the importance of counting the swabs used and why they are always X-ray detectable. We learned about techniques to wash hands properly and why it was recommended to wear two pairs of gloves. After a few weeks we were permitted actually to assist with certain procedures, to be as it were at the cutting edge. But it was Sister Winter, who despite her reticence to be with 'awake patients' taught me the constant need for the nurse always to stand up for, respect and look after those under their care.

12

E.N.T. DERBYSHIRE ROYAL INFIRMARY

GARY'S STORY

Dave Eldergill

E.N.T was an opportunity to extend the skills already gained on the general surgical ward and learn about the post-operative care of some very specific conditions. This was the first time I encountered a patient with a tracheotomy, the first time I learned how to pass a nasogastric tube and the first occasion I had been with a patient to clinic for an endoscopy. It was also the time when I realised how foolhardy it was to wear a tie in a ward environment . Wilfred was an elderly and slightly confused gentlemen who had been sent to our ward for a minor ear procedure. When he had recovered from the anaesthetic, he was due to return to the long-stay geriatric Ward where he been a patient for the previous few months. Rashid, the junior doctor on call, was leaning over the safety rail on the side of Wilfred's bed to ask him how he was feeling. The post-operative haze didn't do anything to make Wilfred less confused and he didn't react well to this smiling face looming over him. Remarkably quickly for someone just waking from a groggy anaesthetic sleep, Wilfred made a grab for Rashid, and placed a vice like grip on the poor doctors tie. He then proceeded to pull Rashid down towards him whilst all the time, the knot on Rashid's tie became like a noose getting tighter and tighter. Luckily, somebody noticed as Rashid had no breath to call for help, and they rushed over and freed the unfortunate houseman from his impending demise. My uniform consisted of a round necked tunic, so no need for the sartorial addition of a tie, but if that ever changed I now had a very good reason not to wear one, and I never did.

Although fit and healthy, Gary was already in the role of a patient, sat on his bed in his pyjamas preparing himself for tomorrow's operation. He was to undergo a procedure to straighten a deviated nasal septum and had been admitted the day before to ensure he remained "nil by mouth" from

82

midnight. He hadn't questioned why he needed to be in his night clothes for the surgeon to be able to examine his nose but just accepted this was how things were done. It was a quiet late shift and after visiting time was over I noticed how excitable he seemed. I sat next to him on the bed, taking a break from going around the ward measuring temperatures, blood pressures and pulses, to find out if he was ok or anxious about the next day. "Did you see who that was over there, visiting that man in the end bed?" he blurted out, almost unable to contain his excitement. I confessed I hadn't and he stated a name I had never heard of before. "Who is that then?" I enquired. He looked at me incredulously as if I must be a complete idiot. "He was part of the team that won the league in 72". I was none the wiser so Gary told me his story.

That was the season I first went to a football match. My parents had no interest at all in football but as a special treat for my tenth birthday in October, my uncle took me to the Baseball Ground to see Derby play Arsenal. All the talk in the school playground had been about Derby County. Up until, then, I had been more interested in playing football with coats for goal posts rather than talking about it, but our local team were on the up. Derby had only lost one match since the start of the season and the schoolboy anticipation was already at fever pitch. Can you imagine how great and important I felt being the centre of attention at school on Monday morning as I recounted again and again, Derby's victory and my part in the heady atmosphere when Hinton scored from a penalty. I had been carried by the surge of the crowd and drowned in the one voice, I was hooked. As that season progressed, school playtimes were spent swapping 'Wonderful World of Soccer Stars' cards, bought in the sweet shop together with a sherbet fountain and a handful of Trebor fruit salad chews. Every ten-year-old boy would pretend that they had been allowed to stay up and watch 'Match of the Day' the previous Saturday evening and never admit they were tucked up in bed after a weekly bath night.

  Following Derby County was pure adrenaline. They were doing well and I was Kevin Hector on the school field. Then towards Christmas a few matches were lost and the pain seemed physical. It was a rollercoaster of emotions as we then began to win again. I didn't see another live match that season. Uncle Bob's generosity did not extend to having a ten-year-old nephew with him regularly in the Pop Side. I though, had become a true fan, I knew every player and I completed Derby County in my sticker album before any other team. May 1972 is a time etched in my consciousness. Our team from an East Midlands town had taken on the big boys of English football and were champions of the First Division. Even though we had beaten Liverpool in the last game of our season, the title was not ours, we had to wait to see the final results for the two chasing teams, Leeds United and Liverpool who both could have snatched it away at the last minute. But they didn't, and the Derby Telegraph went with the headline, "Rams Champions". My Uncle Bob has a copy of that edition framed on his living room wall. That for me was the start of a lifetime's passion, forged in the impressionable mind of a ten-year-old, and it has been with me for my whole life. Since then I've seen highs, including another title in 1975, and terrible lows like when we were relegated to division 3 in the early 1980s. I've seen them play no better than amateur school boys and I've seen them take on and beat the best, but it will always be that first time at the baseball ground that lives forever. Come on you Rams!"

Gary underwent his operation the next morning, first on the list. He recovered very quickly from his anaesthetic and had the packs left in his nose to be removed later in clinic. He saw the surgeon on the ward in the afternoon and was discharged that same evening. Such a brief hospital stay was a new experience for me but was very common on the ENT ward. Over the following years, it has become the norm for many different surgical procedures. It is interesting to see how things change over time, new ways of doing things and new treatments and procedures are being developed all the while. I realise of course, I am now a lot older because my first reaction when encountering anything new in a hospital setting these days is, "They didn't do it like that in my day!"

13

BANK NURSE, DERBYSHIRE ROYAL INFIRMARY

OLIVE'S STORY

To be a student is to have a psychological safety net. Whilst being completely accountable for what we do, there is a sense that in some ways the 'buck stops' with someone else. As a qualified nurse, at whatever level, the process of learning does not stop, one does not suddenly become an expert professional. But even as the most junior member of the ward team, there is a tangible difference in the weight of responsibility that is carried, and even though the process of developing skills and knowledge continues, it is within a very different framework.

My wife began her full-time training as a midwife, so we did a role swap, and that meant that I began working in the 'real world' in the role of a bank nurse. Working on the nursing bank entailed being available to do various shifts, in different locations, to cover shortages of regular staff. I opted to work a few night shifts each week, allowing me to become a Househusband, and part-time nurse. I would be asked by the night sister which duties I could cover and as they were always short of staff there was always a night shift available somewhere in the hospital. I could find myself taking the ward keys following a short handover on a busy medical ward or as second nurse on a quiet, half-full surgical ward. I never knew until I arrived at the hospital where I was going to be or what was going to be expected of me. Work was a constant challenge.

One night shift found me looking after 12 post-operative patients on an ophthalmic ward for minor routine cataract surgery which today would be quite happily performed on a Day Case Unit. Back then, everyone stayed overnight, eye patch in place, and hopefully had a good night's restful sleep before being discharged in the morning. I was expecting a long, quiet night, a chance to catch up with some reading. I would even get a short meal break as the night sister promised to come and take over from me at some stage. It is a nice change not to be busy but the disadvantage is that time can pass very slowly watching the clock until the first dull greys of morning filter through the windows.

At approximately 2.30 in the morning, the ward phone rings and I am at first annoyed, as the patients may be disturbed and that would upset my nice cushy night duty. I rush to answer, hoping somebody has been put through to the wrong location. "Hello this is staff in A&E, we have a patient with a corneal abrasion in his left eye." My first reaction is one of abject horror. I know nothing about eyes, even though I'm the nurse in charge of the ophthalmic ward. In fact, I am the only nurse on the ophthalmic ward, but there is nothing in my training to prepare me for this. I vaguely remember a long afternoon visiting the ophthalmic theatre and trying to stay awake as eyeballs were sliced just beyond my visual range, but that was it. The horror begins to turn to panic as I try to work out what I might actually have to do, when the nurse from A&E continues "Doctor would like to bring him up to treat him in your clinical room: she'll be with you in about five minutes". So not as bad as I first thought, there would be someone else here who should know what they were doing. And so they arrive, the patient pushed by a porter in a wheelchair and the doctor, white coat flapping as she rushed along to keep up and into the brightly-lit clinical room. All the doctor wanted to do was give a topical anaesthetic and antibiotics, place an eye patch over the injury and refer to the consultant the next morning. But when she asks for the Lidocaine Hydrochloride eye drops and the Gentamicin eye drops, I find myself opening every cupboard with no idea of their whereabouts. I am like the proverbial organiser of the brewery party, and I am just getting in the way.

Eventually, after I have unlocked and opened every cupboard, the items are found and administered, and I am then left alone to continue with my unhurried schedule.

On another occasion, I find myself part of the team on a very busy female orthopaedic Ward. This is my first time on this ward so I have the added complication of finding out where things are as well as trying to familiarise myself with the patients. The night goes by at almost a blur, heavy lifting turning immobilised old ladies from one side to the other, admissions from casualty and a constant ringing of the summoning buzzers, with no time to stop and catch a breath until about 4am when it begins to quieten down. Just as I sit down to catch up on paperwork, another buzzer rings so I go down to the bay in question to see what is needed. On a busy ward everything goes at a quicker pace, and as I stride along the corridor I glance at the notes I made during handover. "Joanne, aged 28, R.T.A. (road traffic accident), fracture left femur in traction and awaiting surgery, fracture right humerus in plaster, severe bruising to ribs." Joanne tells me that she needs to use a bedpan. I am a nurse, a professional, so there is no sense of embarrassment as I close the curtains around Joanne's bed. I ascertain how much Joanne can lift herself with her one good arm and realise that I do not need any assistance. I slide the bedpan into position, make sure her buzzer is in reach and say I will return when she is ready. I do this everyday, I am good at projecting a confident, professional manner and Joanne has already been in hospital for quite a while and has overcome any initial awkwardness she may have felt at this intimate procedure. And then the dynamic of the situation changes. "You don't remember me" she says and the veneer of my professionalism slips away. Joanne is a nurse with whom I have previously worked and instantly as she says those words, I recognise her and I feel my face begin to redden. I suddenly feel very uncomfortable. Another nurse goes back later and removes the bedpan and restores Joanne's dignity and bedclothes, and when I go to see her before leaving at the end of my shift, we chat together and laugh about my reaction. I realise that the relationship between nurse and patient is contingent on both parties understanding and agreeing to the condition in which it operates. Context, it seems, is everything.

Sometimes I will have students working with me. I can be challenged about everything I do in the same way as I would have questioned the trained staff when I was a student. Students are a great resource in preventing clinical practice from slipping into a formulaic routine, they keep you on your toes, but I do find myself wondering if I was quite as bolshie when I was in their position.

Working night duties on the nursing bank gives me a lot of time to consider something of what it means to be a nurse. I find myself thinking about the illustrious founder of modern nursing, Florence Nightingale, and her connections with Derby. This is particularly so during the times when I'm sitting at the nurses' station in the subdued lighting of the old-fashioned Nightingale Ward. It is easy to imagine this Victorian lady, gliding in flowing skirts up one side of the room and back down the other, checking on the patient in each bed she passes, with her lamp in hand. My thoughts turn to Olive, a lady I met whilst I was training and the stories she told me of her privileged upbringing as part of a wealthy Derbyshire family. Hers was a family forever connected to Miss Nightingale and her groundbreaking work during the Crimean war.

"I was very fortunate as a child. My family had wealth and privilege and a history that went back generation after generation. During that brief period of peace between the wars we would often go off traveling for extended periods. We went as a whole family, for long vacations visiting the glories of the classical world. It was a little like a twentieth century version of 'The Grand Tour'. We saw Athens and Rome, the Parthenon and the Colosseum. In winter we would ski in Switzerland and summers were often spent in the family home near Nice."

When the world plunged again into darkness, Olive's idyllic youth was over. She joined the WAAF, and had many interesting and daring war time exploits, but it was the stories from the halcyon days of the 1930s she mostly wanted to tell. "I can remember one occasion when we found ourselves in Istanbul tasting the thrill and magic of the East. I even think, if I remember correctly, we had travelled across the continent by train. I didn't know it then but apparently that was the Orient Express. Oh I was a lucky, lucky little girl. During our time there, there was a particular place my father wanted to go and so we all traipsed up to a cemetery overlooking the Bosphorus. He led us to a large memorial cross formed around a circle, almost a silhouette against the blue sky and blue sea. The inscription simply read "Sophia Barnes Nurse April 1855" . "This children", My father declared "is the last resting place of your great grandmother's older sister, an unsung hero of the Crimean war" Sophia was the rebel of her family and like her famous compatriot Florence Nightingale, she had no intention of settling down to a married life of wealth and privilege. She believed that she had a calling on her life, a greater purpose and although it was frowned upon as suitable role for a genteel lady, she travelled to London to work as a nurse. In October 1854 Sophia travelled as one of a party of 38 nurses who accompanied Miss Nightingale on her mission to the sick and wounded soldiers of the Crimean war. The party crossed France from Boulogne to Marseille before boarding a ship to take them the length of the Mediterranean.

The Vectis was an old mail steamer, filthy and uncomfortable and to add to their discomfort, the late autumn Mediterranean weather was appalling. Sophia and all the other nurses arrived on the Asiatic side of what was then still Constantinople in drizzling rain on the 4th of November 1854 ready to begin the Herculean task of treating the casualties of the conflict at the barrack hospital at Scutari. In her letters home, Sophia described the filth and the squalor and the attempts made at introducing a degree of hygiene. She told of cleaning and dressing wounds and how so many more patients died from sickness and disease rather than as a result of their injuries. The letters home ceased after less than a year and eventually the family discovered that Sophia too had fallen victim to an epidemic of cholera. She unfortunately did not survive and was buried in the cemetery next to the hospital together with the many, many patients who never left that far off foreign field. Sophia's story passed into the family's oral history, recounted on dark evenings sat around an open fire, becoming an inspiration to later generations. Olive told me of an aunt who nursed in a field hospital during the Great War, a sister of her grandmother who worked at the Derbyshire General Infirmary in the 1870s before the Royal Infirmary was built. She had a cousin who began her nurse training in Derby just before the outbreak of World War Two and her great niece is currently an ITU sister in Nottingham. There is no statue to Sophia and little written historical record. No great books or films about her exist, and she has no fame like that of Florence Nightingale. But

Sophia was part of the story that contributed to making nursing what it is today and her legacy continues on through the generations of her family who have followed on in her footsteps.

This was how I began my time working as a qualified nurse. I went from ward to ward, speciality to speciality, not restricted to developing specific skills for only one clinical environment. It was nerve-wracking and rewarding in equal measure, and by necessity, I became quite adaptable to new situations. This was also my first opportunity to consider writing as a legitimate means of bringing in some income and was incredibly pleased when an article I wrote on being a part time nurse and working father, was published in the Nursing Standard. It wasn't too long before I missed the stability of being grounded in just one place and so I looked around for something new. I found myself applying for a permanent position in a local care home, still working nights but with the chance to get to know both my patients and my colleagues.

14

OAK VIEW NURSING HOME, DERBY

HAROLD & LILIAN'S STORY

Oak View Nursing Home was a small, private care home situated just off the Derby ring road. It could accommodate no more than 20 residents and had a peaceful, homely atmosphere. When I went to meet the owner, who was also the home's matron, I noticed immediately on going through the large oak front door, the lack of the stale urine aroma that I had noticed permeating the other nursing homes I had already visited. I was going to be interviewed for a job and up until now this was the only place that actually seemed like somewhere I could imagine myself working. Brenda, the owner, was a born nurse. She had dedicated her life to her profession but like so many before her she had to retire when her gradually deteriorating back condition meant that she could no longer cope with the demands of working on a ward. Opening a nursing home was a way of bringing her exacting standards to the private sector and enabled her to keep on doing what she loved best. She was looking for someone to cover a few nights each week, someone she said "who remembers they are working in the residents' home". She also wanted a commitment to providing education for the home's staff, regular talks on the prevention of pressure sores, infection control and anything else that would help her to maintain the high quality of care she expected. When moving from the frantic, hectic bustle of a large NHS hospital to the small, intimate world of a private nursing home, I don't think I could have made a better choice than Oak View.

Harold and Lillian were the oldest residents at Oak View. They were celebrating their platinum anniversary, 70 years of marriage. Sitting to one side of an elaborate cake, they held hands and gazed at each other like a pair of young lovebirds but it still took a leap of the imagination to see these two frail, non-ambulatory nonagenarians, fingers entwined whilst the local paper photographer captured this

95

latest moment for posterity, as the same people that looked back at me from the sepia-toned and time-worn wedding picture from 1921. The young faces gaze back at the camera lens, stiff and formal, nothing candid in the pose. Faces that have a lifetime before them, full of hope and expectation and yet in that presence is the acknowledgment of an absence, of a moment which has been and gone.

Harold and Lillian were together for a lifetime, they had been childhood sweethearts, married in their early twenties and had a rich, full life of experiences. There were Christmases, holidays and also going without in order to save up to put down the deposit for their first home. Once a week wearing Sunday best at church and the annual outing to Skegness. There was a gold watch after 45 years working for the Derby Corporation, first on the trams followed by a long stint in the office and then a whole new career as a caretaker at a school, after retirement. They had faced sickness and health, they had been richer and poorer and they had known peacetime and wartime. One event however was the moment that coloured every subsequent day that followed, the tragic wound that never completely healed. By 1930 the young couple were living with their three children, Thomas aged seven, Betty aged five and the new baby Joyce, in Beaufort Street, Derby. After school one day in the autumn, Thomas had gone out to play with his school friend, George who lived a few doors down on the same road. In a time before PlayStations, computers or even the ubiquitous television, children made their own entertainment. It was the world of Richmal Crompton's 'Just William'. Boys played cowboys and Indians, built dens, lit fires and made go-carts. They came home covered in mud, school blazers ripped and with scuffed knees protruding from short trousers. Parents didn't have to spend every moment worrying about their safety, but perhaps they should have. Thomas and his chum had made their way to a grocers shop on the corner of Chequers Lane and Nottingham Road to get an empty wooden box. The previous day they had been given some wheels from an old pram and with the box they intended to make their very own cart. Children were inventive and Thomas had a real knack putting odds and ends together to make something new. As they made their way back, George full of excited anticipation ran blindly across Nottingham Road and collided with a bicycle, sending both himself and the unfortunate cyclist sprawling into the road. Both were luckily uninjured and picked themselves up, the cyclist, clearly shocked by the incident, spewing obscenities at the boy. Thomas, also running, followed across the road carrying the box and tripped headfirst over the prostrate bicycle. To the absolute horror of the two onlookers, his momentum carried him under the wheels of an oncoming lorry. Thomas suffered head injuries and a broken leg and although taken to the infirmary, died from those injuries shortly after getting there.

The junction of Beaufort Street, Nottingham Road and Chequers Lane was already known locally as "death corner" as there had previously been a number of accidents and fatalities, and the demise of poor Thomas was one more addition to its sad history. No parent expects to bury their children and Lillian struggled to deal with the loss. Harold, of the "stiff upper lip" generation, stoically withdrew, and the lack of communication was nearly the end of the marriage. Time never truly heals but the family gradually adjusted to their new normal, moving away from town to the quite suburb of Mickleover village. They had the two girls and eventually grandchildren, great grandchildren and even the next generation was on the way. Thomas however, forever remained the scruffy, cheeky, impish seven-year-old in their memories, gone but never forgotten.

It was only a few weeks after the celebrations that Harold passed away peacefully in the night. We did not call for a paramedic or an ambulance, as the local GP had been to see him the morning before and he thought that it would not be long before the end came. We made sure that Harold was as comfortable as possible and members of staff took it in turns to sit with them. Lillian lay next to him in their double bed, holding his hand and speaking softly throughout the long night. She knew when he had gone, but her fingers kept their grip around his slowly cooling hand and she carried on speaking the same soothing words until the first subtle light of the day filtered through the curtains. Although no longer mobile, Lillian was a remarkably fit lady considering her very advanced years, and the only medication she took was an occasional paracetamol for pain. Despite this, within two weeks, she too was no longer with us. There was no obvious cause other than that she lost her will to carry on alone. Everything over the last 70 years had been shared and now she was incomplete. They were one soul, connected through both the exquisite joys of the journey and also through the deepest depths of despair. They had laughed together and they had cried together and now as Lillian closed her weary eyes, they remained together.

CONCLUSION

Dave Eldergill

It is a Saturday morning in mid June 1987, it is just before 7am and I am walking from my home, through the city centre to the Derbyshire Royal Infirmary. My route has taken me along Friar Gate, not busy with commuter traffic on a weekend, and up through the pedestrian walkway of St Peter's Street. The city is not yet fully awake and still seems very quiet, some shops open but most not yet ready for the coming day. I make my way past an occasional chip wrapper and a few empty bottles, detritus from the night before, still evident on the ground. As a student nurse on a small salary, I need to pay a mortgage, keep a young family and make sure all the bills were paid so there is nothing left over to enable us to afford a car.

Fortunately our home was within walking distance of all the hospitals where I trained, and this morning's walk would only take me about 20 minutes. This was my first impression of living in a city, albeit quite a small one. I had come from a seaside town in the West Country, used to the constant presence of the sea and the edge of the land which defined the boundaries of my world, and here I was, as far away from the reassuring proximity of the coast as I could possibly be, right in the centre of England. There was a period of adjustment, not only to my new role as a nurse but also to my new location and its people. Daily I would hear the Derby accent, which to my Somerset ear sounded no different from that of Yorkshire or anywhere else up north, but over time I became familiar with "Ey up me duck" and the distinctiveness of the East Midlands pronunciation. I learned that a 'cob' was actually a bread roll and a 'jitty' was in fact an alley way. It was however the people of Derby who would go on to leave the most lasting impression. The individuals I met often had a deep grounding and connection to the place where they lived. I was able to hear their stories, reminiscences which would put the flesh on the bones of my gradually increasing understanding about this landlocked county.

I started this book with the quote from Yan Martel's 'Beatrice and Virgil' in which he says of stories, that they "stitch together the disparate elements of human existence into a coherent whole". During my time in Derby, I encountered many of these individual personal stories and realised how they were also part of a greater tale. Some stories have a definite beginning, middle and end, others we hear, are just a small snippet of something much bigger, which we will never fully know. Stories can run parallel to each other, stories can have crossovers, stories can also come from different ends and then meet in the centre. Some stories seem to exist in isolation and others need their context before we have any idea of what they are about. It is often other people's stories that help us to make sense of our own, seeing our experiences revealed in the light of someone else's. It is those connections with other people that help to define who we are, that give meaning to our own existence and that provide the context for our own ongoing narratives.

History is so much more than just a list of names and dates. It is so much more than an analysis of causes and effects. It is what happened and was experienced by the people who were there, made tangible and real when it is remembered and told, when "those disparate elements of human existence" become "a coherent whole". Here now in the twenty first century, I find it almost unbelievable that I have met and talked to those who recall not just the last century but also the one before that. What tales were they told of what went before and how will the generations that follow add to the tales we tell.?

The context to all of the stories that I have recounted here, has been my experiences whilst nursing. It was an occupation that enabled me to have so many different encounters with such a diversity of people. It is also a profession which has changed dramatically over the last 30 years since I began my training, in some ways for the better and in others not. As part of my research, I once chatted with a nurse who trained at the Royal Infirmary in the late 1930s and during the war years, nearly half a century before me. Joan was a few months short of receiving her telegram from the queen and had a vivid and sharp memory. I learned of her long days and of the matron who ruled with a rod of iron. She showed me the notes she had made, listing the various instruments that she had to get ready for individual surgeons. I was told about how patients died from infection in a time before antibiotics and how the syringes they used to administer injections, were made of glass, not plastic and needed sterilisation before being used again and again. She knew a very different regime from the one under which I worked, and experienced a nurse training programme which in many ways vastly differed from mine and yet we had a connection of more than just our common familiarity with the Victorian buildings we both knew. We were both part of a profession that developed from the key ideas of Florence Nightingale: an understanding that infection control in hospital was essential, that a healthy diet was a necessary part of recovery and that even the design of the hospital buildings had a role to play in a patient's well-being. These are the concepts that have been developed into models of nursing and a highly professional discipline which is very distinct from a solely medical approach. Joan had at the core of her understanding of nursing a sentiment expressed by Florence Nightingale, a sentiment which underpinned my training and one which I know is just as pertinent and relevant today....

"It may seem a strange principle to enunciate as the very first requirement in a hospital that it should do the sick no harm."

FLORENCE NIGHTINGALE

ABOUT THE AUTHOR

Dave Eldergill is an artist and author. He trained as a nurse in Derby in the 1980s and now lives in Somerset.

Printed in Poland
by Amazon Fulfillment
Poland Sp. z o.o., Wrocław